BLAZING
UNCANNY
TRAILS
2

I dedicate this to you.

If you like these kinds of stories, well, so do I, and that's why I wrote them.

Most of these stories were first published by small publishers. I am grateful for their support and ask that you please support them in return, if you can.

A special thank you to David Boop and David Riley for their encouragement, support, and indoctrination into the Weird West.

Thank you to J.A. Campbell and the opportunity to play in her sandbox, the Ghost Hunting Dog/Eye of the Dog world, and for her permission to mention her characters again here in Gasper's story.

*I understand a proposed amendment to the Constitution—which amendment, however, I have not seen—has passed Congress, to the effect that the Federal Government shall never interfere with the domestic institutions of the States, including that of persons held to service. To avoid misconstruction of what I have said, I depart from my purpose not to speak of particular amendments so far as to say that, holding such a provision to now be implied constitutional law, I have no objection to its being made express and irrevocable.*

—Abraham Lincoln
First Inaugural Address
Monday, March 4, 1861

## Warm Springs, North Carolina

## 1867

As my hired carriage rounded the bend in the road, I was awed by the magnificent scope of the amusement park sitting in and among the green trees and the river. I am sure my jaw was agape for at least a half mile as we approached Captain Samjack's Hot Springs, Steam Arcade, and Emporium of Wonder. The carriage ride from Asheville had taken nearly the entire day, and there had been no room for other passengers as I was traveling with a rather large amount of luggage. It was a relief to have the monotony of the ride nearing an end.

Craning my head to peer out the window of my coach, I was treated to the sight of great billows of steam arising out of various places in regular intervals, wonderfully white against the green trees and blue sky. Through the trees I could see over a dozen buildings, half of which were as large as a hotel. Numerous smaller structures were adorned with brightly painted colors I could see from even this distance. I had heard the original hotel, set up for visitors coming to the healing warm springs, was comprised of three hundred and fifty rooms and seated six hundred guests for dinner. I had also heard this was now the smaller of all the lodgings.

As I watched, an airship lazily circled in for a landing in a cleared field with not one, but two hanger bays. Over a dozen men in blue uniforms rushed out to catch the mooring ropes that dangled and traced along the ground. I had to clean the dust off my wire rimmed spectacles to take it all in properly. I would have liked to have come in on an airship, but with my heavy luggage and low income, it hadn't been feasible.

"It's hard to believe that's not actually a city, isn't it?" The carriage driver grinned toothlessly over his shoulder at me. He obviously enjoyed bringing people out here and seeing the look of disbelief upon their faces.

"It is glorious!" I breathed excitedly. I was struck at the number of carriages, wagons, and buggies lined up in neat rows outside a large stable just outside of town. I call it a town, for a town it truly was. What else can a place with accommodations for literally hundreds of people be called? The stable alone appeared to have a hundred horses, and an honest-to-goodness grain-milling style windmill spun in the wind next to the river, right next door to the biggest water wheel I had ever laid eyes upon.

From this distance I couldn't see through the thick trees well enough to take it all in, but I knew it had all been carefully planned out and organized around the river and a large central strolling garden. Captain Samjack had set out to create an international resort destination, and by all accounts, he had successfully done so.

I had to catch my hat as a gust of wind threatened to take it. I pulled my head back inside the carriage and adjusted my jacket and vest, having snagged one of my buttons on the window in my enthusiasm.

"You'll be thinking it even more glorious when I pick you up at the end of your stay." The driver winked at me. "What day should I return for you?"

I admired his tenacity to procure my business beyond this one trip from the train station to Captain Samjack's. It would have worked, had I not already other plans. I had been invited out and offered employ, sight unseen. My reputation had preceded me by much further than I could ever have hoped, and I felt pride as I spoke.

"No need for that. Thank you very much. I will be staying on. I've been hired as a consultant." I'm sure I was unable to hide the excitement in my voice. I expected this engagement to change everything. Since the war, and the death of every close relative, I had been living hand to mouth.

My driver nearly dropped the reigns from his hands. When he turned to look at me again, his mirthful grin had been replaced by genuine concern. His mouth worked silently as he sought words but could not find them. Turning back to the road, he did something most unusual. He stopped the carriage.

Hat in hand, he stepped down out of the dickey box and approached the door by which I sat. He spoke softly and with remorse. "Mr. Henlein, please forgive my boldness." His fat little fingers worked nervously around the edge of his worn hat, twisting the brim and rotating the bowler in circles. He hesitated, searching for the words he wanted to relate.

"My dear sir, please speak freely," I assured him.

He nodded and flashed a nervous smile, again revealing his sparsely embedded teeth. "You see, sir, we in Asheville don't like to speak ill of Captain Samjack's, as it brings in a lot of money to our town." His voice dropped conspiratorially. "But there are rumors."

I chuckled. I enjoyed a good haint story as much as the next fellow and local lore was among my favorite ways to learn more about the peoples to whom I intended to peddle my wares. "Do tell," I encouraged my driver.

"A while back some of the local boys took it on themselves to find out how Samjack's Hell House worked." He must have seen the puzzled look on my face. "The Hell House is one of his mechanical attractions, one supposedly with ghosts haunting it. None of the boys ever returned. Five of them, all gone missing."

"All good haunted houses must have a story behind them," I smiled at him. "I'll be sure to visit."

"Please Mr. Henlein, there is more. You are not the first person I have brought out here to begin a new job. Last year a man by the name of Smythe promised to return to town to pay me, as he lost his wallet somewhere along the way." He nervously ran a hand through his thinning hair. "Now I know there is nothing unusual about a fellow not returning when money is involved, but I sincerely believe he intended to. That was nigh on a year ago, and I have never seen nor heard from him since."

He swallowed hard, eyes flickering to mine, and I nodded to show I was still listening.

"About six months ago, another gentleman, this one by the name of Faber, also promised me he would return, but for a very different reason. He was to return home in two months to wed. He did not return."

I waved my hand towards Captain Samjack's. "Look at the size of this place. With so many people here all the time, people are bound to pass on occasionally."

"His betrothed sent telegrams inquiring, and two men came looking for Faber, but they didn't find him. When they inquired at Captain Samjack's they were told no such person had ever been there. But I know better. I unloaded his luggage myself."

I could not help but smile. It was an excellent scare, a perfect ruse to get me to promise to see him and hire his carriage again. One I enjoyed enough to allow him the pleasure of thinking he had won me over.

"And you would like me to promise you I will return and reassure you I am well, yes?"

"No, sir," he dropped his eyes to the road. "Please do not think me a coward, but I fear if I am involved with any more persons who disappear, people will find me suspect."

I frowned. I hadn't expected that at all. "What would you have of me, then?"

"Please, sir. I ask you do not mention me to anyone, do not let anyone know I mentioned Smythe and Faber… And, please sir, please be very careful, you seem like a nice enough fellow, and I would be greatly relieved to see you back in town one day." He looked away uncomfortably, put his hat back on and climbed back into the dickey box.

With a flick of the reigns, the horses picked up again and our carriage moved forward with a much more somber mood.

My carriage driver surprised me yet again when, after unloading my luggage, he bid me farewell and left, refusing payment. I had to admit, that lent credence to his story in my view.

I was still puzzling this when I was met by the most amazing sight. A free-standing steam powered horse came clip-clopping down the cobblestone road towards me, pulling a small one-seated wagon behind it. There were dozens of people strolling around the grounds and they all stopped to watch as it passed. Gleaming golden brown in the sunlight, the metal creature had been polished brightly and was a joy to behold.

A dashing middle-aged gentleman in a fine suit and top hat drove the wagon, and he smiled and waved jovially to the pedestrians as he passed them. He was immaculately groomed, and his curled mustache would have been the envy of any carnival barker. Several persons returned his wave, smiles upon their faces.

The wagon stopped at the intricately designed wrought iron entrance gate, and the metal horse blew steam out of its nostrils at me. I stared in amazement, the conversation with my carriage driver completely forgotten.

"Peter Henlein, I presume." The driver looked down at me from where he had been steering the machine. It appeared he had been using levers rather than reigns. Somehow the motions were being transferred through the hitch and to the mechanism.

"I am," I nodded back with a grin on my face. I was enraptured with the mechanical horse twitching its metal ears and swishing its horse-hair tail at nonexistent flies. "May I touch it?"

"Of course!" The man climbed down and patted the faux animal solidly, causing the metal to ring under his hand. "My pride and joy! Not very practical, but a joy nonetheless. A favorite of the guests, too. Unfortunately his boiler is very small by necessity, and he is not good for more than an hour. Also," his voice dropped conspiratorially, "he trips on anything larger than a small stone. I'm still working on that."

He walked around the front of the automata as I ran my hands down the smooth metal. A burnished brass of some sort, I guessed. The craftsmanship was among the finest I had ever seen. The seams and welds sealed tightly and were smoothed so well I could hardly locate them. The nostrils blew steam again and snapped me out of my absorption.

I realized the man was standing patiently next to me. "Oh, my! I am so sorry. How very rude of me." I offered my hand in greeting. "Peter Henlein."

"Mathias Samjack, Captain of the Research Division of Engineers of the Union Army, retired." He shook my hand firmly. Under his white cotton glove I thought I felt something not unlike a metal gauntlet, but surely I was mistaken, as his hand was no bulkier than normal. "No apologies necessary. It is a thrill to see a fellow enthusiast so excited about my craft."

"Pleased to make your acquaintance, Captain. I had heard of the marvels you have here, but I was ill prepared for just how exquisite your workmanship is!"

"Please! You flatter me, and I thank you kindly, but I cannot take all of the credit. There are over a hundred metal workers and artisans here who work very hard at making my dreams come true. Come! I will show you the wonders we have created, the wonders that keep me dealing with an average of over a thousand guests at any one time." He grabbed the largest piece of my luggage and loaded it effortlessly into the carriage.

I was awed by the man's strength and vitality as he hefted the last two pieces of luggage before I could finish with the single piece I had secured. I caught him enjoying my admiration out of the corner of my eye and he winked convivially at me.

Raising a white gloved hand and waving, Captain Samjack called over a porter I hadn't noticed standing beside the gate. Four more stood in the shade of a waiting area set just inside the gate. All were handsome young Coloreds dressed in sharp blue uniforms with blue fezzes and gold trim. I wondered if the passing resemblance to the military uniforms of the North was intentional.

"Ovid, please take Mr. Henlein's luggage to his quarters and see to it everything is prepared for his arrival. I will give him the tour, and we should be there in an hour or so." Captain Samjack treated the porter with more respect than I expected from a man of his station.

Ovid nodded politely and hopped up onto the buckboard of the wagon. With an expert flip of levers and pedals, the man-made equine again came to life and began trotting down the cobblestone road, its striking hooves sounding with an echoing ring. Again, people stopped to watch it pass by, wonder and joy in their eyes.

"I was glad to hear you were a man from the North, Mr. Henlein. I employ many Coloreds here, and I treat them all as I would anyone else." Captain Samjack began strolling farther into the amusement park as he spoke. "I have found them to be exceptionally hard workers and extremely grateful for the opportunity to start a new life. The world has become a difficult place for them since the end of the war. I tell you this bluntly, as, if you have a problem with that, now is the time to decide perhaps this is not the place for you."

"Uh, no, of course not."

Samjack nodded. "Setting up this side of the Mason-Dixon Line was perhaps not ideal, but I came for the steam energy I could harness from the hot springs. I discovered it not too far from the warm springs people have been using for medicinal purposes for a hundred years."

"Is it truly that hot?" I was amazed steaming water would come from the ground.

"Unfortunately, no, but it is hot enough to be useful. Certainly we are never cold around here in the winter. After the hardships of the war, that is no small blessing. But please, you have only just arrived. It would be prudent for me to welcome you properly before regaling you with war stories." He grinned wide.

I found myself liking this man. Not only were his interests in tinkering parallel with mine, I found him to be forthright and amiable.

As we began strolling onto the grounds, I was taken by the quality of fashion worn by the visitors. It reminded me of illustrations I had seen of Londoners parading around. I had never thought to actually see so many well-to-do persons. I began to feel quite self-conscious about my own frayed attire.

"What is your opinion on the place of a Colored in this new world? Should an ex-slave be allowed to sit on a jury and judge you as one of your peers? Should an uneducated Colored man be elected as President, or be allowed to represent our country as a diplomat?"

Captain Samjack's question caught me by surprise. It seemed a very heavy concern for such an idyllic place.

I stuttered in my answer. "These are not questions I have fully considered, Captain. Are they relevant?"

"Extremely. You should begin considering them now. The world has changed, and more change is to come. And that is why I have asked you here. To be a part of that change, to help me change the world with my mechanics, my power, my engineering. Since the first horologists, man has been struggling to master the gear, the lever, the spring, and through those tools…the universe itself. And we have it all within our grasp right here!" Samjack's eyes were wide and wild with a fierce joy as he looked at me to see if I shared his enthusiasm.

My eyes must have been lacking, for his enthralled grin faded quickly.

"I get ahead of myself!" He used a voice I thought might contain false levity. "I have yet to show you the wonders we have achieved so that I may convince you of those we are going to achieve. See here." He strayed to the side of the road and waved his hand at a magnificent circular contraption with carved wooden horses mounted upon it.

"This is a carousel based upon descriptions of similar things in Europe. Except mine is powered by neither human nor beast, but steam. It is quite a simple amusement, really, and by far the simplest construct we have here. It does little more than go in a circle, but the ladies are ever so pleased with riding upon it.

"For the more adventurous young men, I devised a different type of carousel altogether. I got the idea while I was working to reduce the speed of this one to a leisurely pace. You can see it right over there, between those trees." He pointed as we walked towards it. "The principle is exactly the same, but rather than spinning the entire platform, I built train tracks and put cars upon them. The same mechanism I used for the first carousel is used to spin the cars around in circles upon those tracks but at a much higher rate of speed. I then added a few bumps to the tracks, and had an instant hit with the young men."

We walked on as he continued to show me some of the wonders he had built, and explained how each one led to the ideas and the technology behind creating the next. There was a small river continuously flowing in a wide irregular circle around the grounds, upon which passengers could take a relaxing ride in small two-person boats. A large set of swings set upon a giant Maypole spun riders in a wide arcing circle. A puppet wagon with marionettes that performed by themselves, with no human operating the strings. An arcade with games of chance that whirred and clicked, rang, and rattled, while bouncing balls or coins around inside them.

My head spun with the ingenious wonders around me, I could hardly keep up as he pointed out the workshops, the main lodgings, and the worker's living quarters, where I would be staying.

"All of my workers stay here," Captain Samjack eyed me for a reaction. "Including the Coloreds. I have no separate facilities."

"And why should you?" I asked, deducing the reaction he wanted from me, but not knowing what he was expecting me to say. Apparently my reaction was good enough, for he moved on towards the doors.

"So, Mr. Henlein, now that I have shown you some of my wonders, I would like be so forward as to ask you to share yours." Captain Samjack's face was earnest and his excitement was contagious. That made me feel better, as it was what I had come here for.

"I would be delighted. Where can I set up?"

Captain Samjack surprised me by having a large glass display case ready in one of his exhibition halls. As part of my new employment, he offered to rent my attraction for the duration of my employ, effectively doubling my pay.

"I hope you do not feel it presumptuous of me," he said, "but I do believe, if your circus is the magnificent creation I have been told it is, my customers—our customers—will be enthralled with it."

"Of course. I'm thrilled. It has been my passion to show it to people. And not just because they pay me to see it." I grinned. "However, I find it hard to believe my work would be worthy of display alongside these marvels." I gestured towards the other displays that had nearly taken my breath away.

One held a replica of the Euphonia Talking Machine, complete with the eerily realistic, yet dead-not-dead, disembodied woman's face, that moved and spoke as Captain Samjack worked the keyboard that brought it to unsettling, inhuman, life.

"Four score and seven years ago…"

At Captain Samjack's will, the words of President Lincoln's famous speech filled the air, emanating from a machine. The voice was reedy and sounded as though it echoed up from the depths of hell, but the words were clear and articulate. Enough so as to stand my hair on end.

"…our fathers brought forth on this continent, a new nation, conceived in Liberty, and dedicated to the proposition that all men are created equal."

The original machine had been destroyed by its creator a decade earlier, and I had never thought I would set eyes upon such a wonder. I never even thought to ask how a replica had been created. My fascination with the machine was rivaled only by my relief when Captain Samjack stopped manipulating the controls and the bellows blew a last unearthly breath through the supple lips on that uncanny mouth. I couldn't help but wonder if the horrific almost-life of Joseph Faber's creation had been a factor in the ending of his own.

Other displays around us held automata that could draw, write, and play instruments, but none were as disquieting as Euphonia Talking Machine. I wasn't sure anything could be.

"Imagine a world," Samjack said, "where we can send messages via telegraphy using machines like this to translate them to the masses! The common man would no longer need to wonder at, or be at the mercy of, the translation of others. It would be nearly as good as hearing the sender's own voice."

"I have heard tell of an invention that does transmit the actual sound of the voice," I said, trying not to imagine a soulless face speaking, with a haunting sepulchral voice, to the people from the corners of all the city streets. I began unpacking my display to move my thoughts away from the disturbing idea. "It was invented by an Italian gentleman. Manzetti, if I recall correctly. He calls it a speaking telegraph."

Captain Samjack waved his had dismissively. "The words are garbled and difficult to understand. It is of no real use for communication if you can't understand what is being said. It is promising for the future, though, I admit."

Looking over my shoulder as I finished the final touches on my setup, Samjack commented on the speed with which I had been able to assemble my flea circus.

"Repetition has improved my ability, but necessity deemed I find faster ways to set up and take down. Not all places are as friendly as they first seem."

"Very true." Samjack twisted at the corner of his black mustache as he appeared to be resisting the temptation to touch my miniatures.

"There. All done. Now all I need to do is catch some fleas, and it is ready."

Captain Samjack gave me a startled look. "I was under the impression your flea circus was entirely mechanical."

"Oh, it is," I assured him. "But people always look for the fleas, so I provide them, extraneous though they are."

"If it is acceptable with you," he stood up and straightened his jacket, "I would prefer our customers see the technology we are capable of. I would rather they knew there were no fleas."

"Well, of course. If that is what you would like." I was confused. Most people preferred the illusion I had trained the fleas.

"I would. Your skills in miniaturization are what led me to you."

"In that case, please allow me to demonstrate." I released the stop lever on the back of the platform base, and the miniature circus came to life.

Tinny music emanated from the music box I had built into the inch-long carnival organ wagon. As the brightly colored music machine began to move around the platform, its miniscule brass pipes moved up and down rhythmically.

The red and white Big Top unfolded itself, turning from a small pile of fabric and rods into a tent no larger than a watermelon, encompassing half of the display. Rods holding the tightrope and the trapeze snapped up into place and the tiny unicycle began crawling across the tightrope, the trapezes began swinging, and the clown wagon began doing irregular laps around the arena.

A strongman weight set rose and fell on nearly invisible wires while a tiny cannon shot out a ball that slowly rolled back and reloaded itself.

"Oh. I almost forgot." I pulled out a small flask of water and added it to the basin below the high dive. Almost immediately a drop of water jumped from the basin as though a flea had plunged into it and sent out a splash.

Imaginary vendors made of nothing more than painted metal boxes the size of rice grains walked between the stadium seats, selling nonexistent roasted nuts and ale. A tiny brass lion opened and closed its mouth inside a cage while a miniature chair moved around it.

"That's my lion tamer," I told Samjack as he leaned in close to look.

"Magnets?" he asked.

"Yes. I have separate rotating discs underneath with multiple magnets on each to simulate the random movement of the chair."

"And the vehicles are magnetic also?" He sounded disappointed as he pointed to the clown wagon, the fancy carriage, and the circus train running around the perimeter on a track.

"Only partially. They have magnets inside them to shut them off with my main control lever, but individually they are all clockwork. They have to be wound every twenty minutes or so." I moved the main lever back to the stop position and everything stopped moving. I picked up the clown car and its wheels immediately began turning again. I handed it to Samjack.

He held it up to his eye and turned it around. It was not much larger than his thumbnail. "Your attention to detail is commendable. You truly are an artist. I do not see a keyhole, how do you wind it?"

"I chose not to have a key. I display my circus in many dusty areas, and the dirt is damaging and difficult to clean out. Once one of my toys becomes dirty, cleaning it is nearly as much work as building a new one. So I contrived a keyless way, a slip gear on the wheels, allowing me to wind it like so." I lightly put a finger on the organ car and rolled it backwards an inch. The internal spring and gears clicked. "A second slip gear prevents over winding." I continued to roll it backwards, demonstrating the clicking sound.

"How ingenious! The information that came to me regarding your skill was quite accurate. I am most pleased." He sat the clown wagon back on the platform and admired the scene for a moment before nodding his head in what I hoped was satisfaction. "Well, I am quite sure I have occupied your time a bit too much since your arrival. I shall leave you to your own means for the evening. Someone will come around to fetch you for dinner. Meanwhile, please feel free to look around and take advantage of the amusements."

With a nod of his head and a tip of his hat, my new benefactor left me to my own devices.

It was with great pleasure that I wandered through the immaculately tended grounds. As the night fell, it transformed into a fantasy wonderland. Glass orbs of light illuminated pathways like will-o-wisps caught in jars. I had heard of Joseph Swan's electric light, but I had never seen one. It amazed me all the more to see hundreds of them, as though the stars had been brought down from the heavens and set free into the gardens. The appearance was nothing at all like gas lights, in color or illumination. The light seemed sharper, crisper somehow, and it cause the shadows to seem deeper, and more defined.

I enjoyed the attention to the grounds as much as the masterful metalworking I had seen, and the use of the lighted globes to create an air of mystery was an experience I found to be unmatched in my life. It was there, in the gardens, I encountered a comely young lady quietly sobbing in a secluded gazebo. The gazebo itself was yet another magnificent work of metal craftsmanship, lit by a solitary bulb that cast entrancing geometric shadows, and I had been approaching to inspect it when I happened upon the distraught woman.

"Oh! I am terribly sorry, miss. I did not mean to intrude. I didn't realize anyone was here." I bowed slightly in apology and backed out of the gazebo.

"No. It is my fault. Please, come in. I should be going anyway." She dabbed at her nose with a handkerchief.

Then I noticed her garments were not the finery of the other people guesting here. In fact, they were as plain as my own. I had been feeling a bit out of place myself and suspected this might be what had brought the lady to tears. I had seen no other

14

person, not even those in employ, wearing clothing as worn or plain as those this woman and I wore.

She must have noticed my clothing as well. "Oh! Do you work here? I don't believe I have seen you before." She stood up quickly to follow me out into the open.

"Well, I suppose I do." I had been told I would be employed here, at any rate.

"Did you ever meet a man named William Faber? He would have arrived here around six months ago. He's a rather large man, with dark hair and blue eyes." Her words were rushed and sounded more desperate than I am sure she would have liked. "He is a steam engineer. He specializes in improving the designs of—"

"No, ma'am. I have just arrived this very day. I have actually yet to start my employ." I interrupted her as her voice worked towards a fever pitch. As I spoke the words, I recognized the name she had used. Faber. The man my carriage driver had spoken of.

"Oh. I am terribly sorry to have bothered you," she half gasped, half sobbed.

I watched, dumbstruck, as she hurried away into the gardens.

I pulled the fountain pen back from the page. The solicitor hardly waited for my signature to dry before he snatched the employment contract away and vanished out of the room. I had never seen the like of the contract, full of confidentiality clauses, patent protections, and ownership claims. I supposed Captain Samjack had good reasons for them, but they were extremely harsh, imposing penalties that, in my opinion, could be likened to bonded labor.

I said as much to Captain Samjack as we rose from the meeting table.

"Nothing more than necessary precautions, I assure you. Many of the things we work with here were developed during the war, and it would be best to keep them to ourselves. Nothing we would want a foreign army to lay hands upon, hey?" His answer seemed a bit too cavalier, perhaps even rehearsed to my ear, but his smile was a genuine as ever.

I tried not to think about Faber and one particular clause I had read that stood out in my mind: any person terminated from employment for wrongdoings would not be recognized as having ever worked here.

"Come!" Captain Samjack stood and fetched his top hat. "Now that it is official, I wish to show you my crowning achievement, and the reason why I need your help."

"I assume it is for small work." I referred to my ability for miniaturization as I followed suit.

"Of course it is! But not so much that I need you to do it, per say, as I want you to figure out how it can be done."

"Generally, anything can be done on a smaller scale. You merely need to create smaller parts."

"Generally, yes," Samjack agreed as he led me out into the grounds. The morning was exquisite, and guests were taking their breakfasts out of doors on lawn furniture. "But not always. I have tried reducing the size of a steam engine, a feat not too complicated in and of itself, but then you still have to deal with the problems of fuel and the boiler, and things get much more difficult."

I nodded as I walked. "That is why I chose to go with clockwork on my miniatures. So I wouldn't have to refuel and replace the water every few minutes."

As Captain Samjack led me across the grounds a porter came running up and stopped smartly in front of him. I swear I almost thought the man was going to salute, so disciplined did he seem to be.

"Report." Samjack's voice and attitude reflected his military background and enhanced the illusion the porter was a soldier.

"'Nother wagon full arrivin', uh…" the colored man flicked his eyes nervously towards me, "…Captain." He finished his sentence as though he had wanted to call Samjack something else.

Samjack had already expressed his opinions in the matters of the Coloreds to such a degree I was given cause to wonder if this man had a familiarity with the captain that was hidden from the guests to prevent awkward questions. I had to admit, if he would have called Captain Samjack 'Mathias' I would have been taken aback by the informality.

"See they are properly welcomed and taken care of," the captain instructed.

The porter nodded and returned the way he had come in a jog.

"More Coloreds coming in looking for work," Samjack informed me as we resumed walking. "Once word got out I would hire them at a decent wage, they have been coming in by the wagon load on a regular basis. Close to fifty a week, on average."

"That's a lot of men. I have seen a lot of people in your employ here, but fifty new hires a week? Do you employ them all?"

Samjack laughed. "No. Of course not. There are way too many. We do have over five hundred support staff to take care of the guests alone, and I have nearly a thousand employees all together, but even with so many positions to fill, I do not have fifty vacancies a week. I send many of them on to the farms and mines that supply us. I imagine most of them find what they are looking for."

We arrived at a building I hadn't seen the night before, a building unlike any of the others on the grounds. The name was emblazoned in carved stone letters across the top. Captain Samjack's Hell House.

It made me think of the five youths my carriage driver had mentioned.

Although no larger than a typical building, it was shaped to look like a medieval castle, replete with gargoyles and other grotesque beasts carved into the architecture. No bright colors here. No promises of wonders to behold inside. It looked forbidding and distinctly unwelcoming with spear tipped fencing and a murky moat around it. The lowered drawbridge looked like a sickly tongue to the raised portcullis' fang-like teeth. The foliage around the castle, which I call it for no other term seems to fit, was healthy but had been carefully chosen to be of varieties that appeared wilted and droopy, adding to the sense of foreboding doom and death within.

"Our most controversial amusement," the captain waved a white gloved hand at it as we crossed the wooden drawbridge into the gaping maw. "Some can't get enough of it; others can't bring themselves to enter. Have you been?"

I shook my head as he unlocked a hidden side door to the left of the main entrance.

"You should. It is most terrifying indeed." He winked at me rakishly. "If I do say so myself."

As we entered the side door, I was surprised to find the interior lit by the same type of electric lights I had been entranced by in the garden. It had never occurred to me that I would see such a sight—the expenditure of energy it must have taken to light the interiors of buildings during the daylight hours boggled my mind.

It only took my eyes a moment to adjust to the new light, and when they had, I found I could see perfectly well.

"Until recently, our lights were powered by our waterwheel," the captain said as he noticed me looking at them. He led me through a corridor that seemed to circle the perimeter of the building. Passing several heavy wooden doors with iron shuttered viewports in them, he whispered, "Those are for our guests' safety. We can peek in on them from here and go in if needed."

Intrigued by an attraction that might require patrons to be rescued, I raised the shield on one of the doors and peeked but saw only blackness beyond.

There was a final door at the end of the passage. Samjack unlocked it with a heavy iron key and revealed a stone stairway leading downwards. Cool air drifted up from below and more lights illuminated the way. He started down the stairs and I followed, shutting the door behind me and locking it when he motioned for me to do so. He stopped halfway down the stairs and turned to look at me earnestly.

"I normally would bring you into what we are doing at a more manageable pace, but I am quite anxious to move on past some setbacks we have had. Please forgive me. And please be prepared to accept what you are about to see as real." He continued down the stairs, leaving me to ponder what more could there possibly be in this place of wonders.

I hurried after him and found myself, instead of in a cellar, at the junction of several tunnels, each with a string of lights showing the way through the darkness. The tunnels appeared to be roughhewn out of the rock of the Earth itself. Tracks had been laid down in the tunnels, presumably to run minecarts upon. They came out of each of the tunnels and intersected here, joining into one track that continued on in the direction that, I thought, would lead under the Hell House.

Samjack stepped smartly over the tracks and headed into the tunnel on the left. "A true underground railroad," he called over his shoulder at me. "One I tried to expand, but the water tables here did not cooperate. I had envisioned running supplies up from here, coming in under the lodgings, so the guests would never see the food or workers come and go. Unfortunately, one can't have everything. Mind the pipes, they can be fragile."

I looked down to where he pointed. Alongside the tracks ran pipes I presumed carried the water for his steam powered amusements above ground. I stepped over them and followed Samjack as he continued speaking about the problems with the varying water tables in this area.

His voice began to echo as the tunnel opened up into a cavern. Throughout the room, the electric light bounced off large white stalagmites and stalactites. I was awed. The room was nearly the size of the hotel above ground, not only in expanse, but in height as well. We followed the tracks as they wove around the largest formations. Sparkles shone in the electric light as we walked past gardens of what appeared to be milky diamonds and crystalline straws.

"I found this room quite by happy accident not too long after finding the hot springs," Samjack continued. "I was appropriately amazed and impressed, as you look to be, but then I found this room…"

He stepped through an opening made only wide enough for the minecarts and I followed him into the greatest room I have ever seen or heard of. A cavern large enough I could see what appeared to be a cloud of haze hanging in the air above the middle of it. The light from the guiding electric bulbs failed to reach to the far side of the cavern, leaving it shrouded in mystery darker than the darkest night.

The ground we walked upon had been worked and smoothed, removing most of the natural formations, but from what I could see of the ceiling in the dim light stalactites the size of trees hung above our heads in an inverted forest.

Stores of barrels and crates, and piles of raw materials, metals, and coal lined the cavern wall. There were enough crates to supply a whole town with whatever was in them, which I supposed he was doing as he had nearly a thousand guests above our heads. The cool temperature down here was ideal, making this the largest root cellar I had ever heard of.

"As you can see, once I found this room, I had little need for the other."

"Will the wonders never cease?" I mused aloud, entranced by the enormity of it all.

Samjack chuckled. "Oh, I still have one for you."

It took us over ten minutes to cross the gargantuan cave, even following the flat, mostly straight, path of the minecart tracks. The only times the tracks deviated were to wind around pillars of solid stone the size of oak trees. The stones sparkled in the electric light, showing a deep composition of materials I couldn't begin to guess. My eyes were so wide with wonder I don't think I spoke the entire time.

As we rounded yet another man-made wall of crates and barrels, we passed men in blue uniforms who were working at stacking metallic objects into neat piles. I thought I recognized what the men were stacking.

"Are those breastplates? Are you making suits of armor?" I asked.

"Close enough. We are in the final stages of mass-producing automatons. Not mere curiosities such as we have on display above, but truly autonomous. They will be capable of navigating on their own, without being steered. They will be able to hear orders given to them, and answer back in intelligible speech with a miniature version of the Euphonia Talking Machine. We have perfected and miniaturized nearly everything we need."

"Nearly everything?" The words seemed to stumble out of my mouth on their own accord as my brain attempted to keep up with what Samjack had said.

"That, my dear sir, is where you come in." We had finally reached the far side of the cavern, and he directed me up a staircase.

"I didn't really need to bring you this way, but it is such an impressive walk I couldn't resist." Captain Samjack smiled with obvious pride.

"Quite impressive, indeed." I was still in awe, not only of the cavern but of Samjack's revelation of automatons, as I reached the top of the stairs and opened the door. It opened into a factory of some sort. At least two dozen workbenches were lined up in neat rows, each with tools all carefully placed upon them, ready to be used.

"My greatest surprise for you lies in that room." Captain Samjack's voice was somber as I had ever heard it. "I ask you to think carefully about it as you perceive it for the first time."

He opened the door and I stepped in.

A great silver metal construct filled the room, in the shape of a sphere flattened at both the top and bottom. At first, I thought it a giant boiler. But then I noticed the blur of motion around the equatorial circumference and the giant gear wheel spinning rapidly next to it.

The gear was connected to teeth spinning around the outside of the construct. In turn, the wheel spun several more gears and pulleys which, also in turn, spun off again to other things, moving and turning them.

I realized I was looking at a giant motor of a design unlike any I had ever seen.

Circling it, I attempted to ascertain how it was working, and I realized there was no source of power to the motor. At least no source I could see. No pipes bringing anything in, no exhaust pipes letting anything out. No ash cleanout or coal bin.

Perhaps the fuel source came up from below, I thought, but that would be a rather impractical design. So I looked up top, but found nothing.

Bemused, I looked at Captain Samjack. He was bouncing on his toes in excitement.

"Well?" he asked with childish delight.

"I am embarrassed to admit, you have confounded me as to not only your fuel source, but as to exactly what type of motor this is."

"This, Mr. Henlein, is a perpetual motion engine."

The design of the engine was genius, and I now understood why Samjack had insisted upon his secrecy clauses in the employment contracts. As I worked upon my own private bench in my own private workroom, trying to find a way to miniaturize his design, I realized Samjack was going to be a very famous and very rich man. Well, more famous and rich than he already was, anyway. And his boasting upon our first meeting, of mastering the universe itself, was not quite so farfetched as it had first seemed. What couldn't be done with unlimited power?

The hard part was finding even more ways to use it. Obviously, it could be used to power everything that had already been done with other power sources, but what more could we achieve?

Samjack's electric lights were among the simplest of the ideas, and he had already managed to shrink the design of the motor small enough to power individual carriages. It was an absolute delight when he allowed me to drive his prototype, well out of sight of his guests, of course.

His biggest problem, other than shrinking the motor even smaller, was disengaging and re-engaging the gears. Doing so was hard on the gears and tended to wear them out quickly, defeating the purpose of an unlimited maintenance-free engine. I pondered these fantasies as I worked.

At some point I became aware someone had been bringing me food. I hadn't been aware I had been eating, so engrossed had I become in my part of the work. Once I caught myself in the adjacent latrine still working. I probably wouldn't have noticed had I not dropped the part down the privy hole.

Finally, when my eyes were too dried out to see any longer, I realized I had to stop and rest. I had already napped at my workbench, but with the electric lighting, there was an illusion of no passage of time, and the nap had been as unrestful as it had been unintentional.

Stretching my sore bones, I stumbled outside towards the living quarters. The sun was bright and burned at my eyes.

"Ah! There you are." Captain Samjack's voice came at me through the glare. "How are you managing? Four days is a long time to go without respite."

"Four days?" I was shocked.

Samjack laughed. "They told me you were not aware of them when they came and went with the food. I see that was true. Have you made much headway?"

I rubbed my eyes. "In truth, I am tired enough I cannot say. You are welcome to look in on the bench…"

"Of course not! I would never impose upon a master at work. Make sure you keep your health up and keep me appraised—when you remember to, of course." He gave me that roguish wink of his and continued past me.

I smiled back at him but he was already gone.

Continuing on, I was stopped by yet another voice, a feminine one this time.

"Oh, hello again."

I squinted at the face, but it was the clothing my tired eyes recognized. The woman from the gazebo, the one who had been looking for…Forbes? Farady? What was his name? I could not believe how tired I was.

"Madam," I took my hat off and bowed a greeting.

"I never got a chance to apologize to you for my unseemly behavior the other night." She demurely looked away. "I am dreadfully sorry. You ought not to have seen me like that." She hesitated and examined me more closely. "Are you all right?"

Her face blurred in my vision.

"I am dreadfully tired, Madam, please excuse my unsteadiness. I was headed to my room."

"Please, allow me to be so bold as to help you." She put a steadying hand on my elbow. "Shall I call for a servant?"

"Oh, no. I'm quite all right." I don't recall what happened next.

I awoke in the softest bed with the smoothest sheets. It must have been made for royalty. It felt so good I didn't dare move and disturb the dream. I stayed still and refused to come back out into the real world.

I could hear soft voices from far away. One was a woman's voice. It had been a long time since I had awoke to the sound of a woman's voice; since before the war, before my mother died.

"You will summon me when he does awaken?" Captain Samjack's voice. I recognized it from my dreams of magnificent mechanical creations.

"Of course. He was so weak it will take him a while. I would guess he hadn't had any water in days." It was the woman's voice.

She was probably right. I vaguely recalled eating at my workbench, but I didn't remember drinking anything.

"That would be my fault. I had servants checking on him and bringing him food, but I did not consider drink. I owe you a debt of gratitude for assisting him, Madam. Thank you."

"It is the least I could do, after you have been so kind as to let me stay here."

"I will stay close and keep checking in, sir. The lady can send me after you with any news." A third voice, another man.

Something else was said, but I missed it over the ruffle of my silk sheets as I rolled over. I heard the door shut and boot steps depart down the hallway.

"Do you think he did something to the poor man?" The woman's voice was whispered.

"No. Talk is he's waiting for whatever that man is working on, and wants it bad. I haven't been able to find out what it is. I think Samjack is getting close, and this man is helping him get there."

"I don't know how to find out about it unless he talks in his sleep." The woman's voice was exasperated. "If I ask any more questions of people, Samjack is likely to make me disappear, too."

"I know." The man's voice sounded just as tired. "I'm starting to wonder if we should kill Samjack and get this whole thing over with."

"I've had the same thought. We should think on it more before we do anything hasty. Go on and see if anyone is talking now, and I'll go see if our guest talks in his sleep."

I settled myself in and feigned sleep as I heard the door open and close again. In a moment I could hear the rustle of the woman's skirts next to my bed. A cold wet cloth startled me when it touched my forehead. I moaned to cover up my reaction.

"Oh, you poor dear," the woman muttered under her breath. "What is that man doing to you poor people?"

I doubted I could feign sleep very long, so I gave up my ruse and opened my eyes. "Probably not plotting to kill us," I said.

"Oh!" She jumped back, startled. Her face went hard. "You heard that?"

I realized I was looking into the eyes of the woman who had been searching for her lost betrothed. "Yeah. I heard. Why would you want to kill Samjack? Do you really believe he killed your fiancée?"

I sat up in the bed. Her eyes were so wild I was worried what she might do. She seemed to reach a decision.

"I guess my deception is exposed. Either that or I could kill you, but I am not in the habit of killing innocents." She sat on the corner of the bed, far enough away I couldn't reach her, yet close enough I believed what she was saying.

"My name is Mary Stewart. I work for the Pinkerton National Detective Agency."

I stared at her. "And that gives you the right to plot murder?"

"No." She looked away unhappily and then looked back. "I find murderers. And Samjack…" she pursed her lips as she searched for words. "The Pinkertons were hired to investigate President Lincoln's assassination. There were things about it that didn't add up. Oh, there was a great conspiracy," she forestalled my question, "but it was set up to hide something else. Something we have followed back here to Samjack."

"You think…" I couldn't get the words out. The idea Captain Samjack would have assassinated Lincoln was ludicrous.

"We do. And many more on top of that. Samjack was notorious for prisoners of war disappearing under his care, and since I have been here, I have seen a couple hundred Coloreds come in and not a single one go out. I know all about the farms and the mines he supposedly sends them to, but when the Pinkertons looked into it, they found less than two hundred men who had been sent on from here. I'm starting to wonder where all the newly freed slaves are going."

"But he…" My mind was in a whirl. "But Samjack…" I didn't even know what I wanted to say.

Mary waited for my words, but when they didn't come she spoke again. "I have been forthcoming with you. I cannot control what you do with this information, but I beg of you, look around you. Tell me you see nothing wrong here, that everything feels like it is exactly as it seems."

I could not. I had to admit a few things had felt out of kilter, but nothing I could, or even would point my finger at.

"I see you thinking. You know." Mary coaxed me. "You are in a position to help us. Tell us what you know."

"Aha!" I chuckled. "So you want the secrets. Sorry. I signed my life away saying I would not reveal them, and I only know the one anyway, and it is nothing you are looking for."

"I'm glad to hear your integrity is intact." Captain Samjack stepped out of the closet with a pistol leveled at Mary. He was followed by two men with placid expressions who also held pistols. "Unfortunately, I can no longer trust your motives, Mr. Henlein. That is a grave disappointment to me."

At gunpoint we were put into the secret passageway in the closet and taken through dark corridors until I had no idea where we were. At Samjack's orders I was blindfolded, bound, gagged, and then lifted by two men into a metal box. I listened intently as Mary continued to argue with Samjack.

"If you are going to kill me, at least do me the courtesy of explaining why you had Lincoln killed. I have spent two years in the pursuit of trying to figure it out, and am now giving my life. I would really like to know." Mary sounded proud and brave. I wished I would have said something brave.

After a long pause, Samjack answered. "I do this courtesy as a last request, as you are an unfortunate pawn in this game and could not know what you got yourself into.

"Lincoln was a capitulator. He created a platform against slavery, and when he was elected he didn't want to do anything about it. It took me a lot of work to start that war, and I made damn sure he had to fight it. And then, at the drop of a hat, he accepts the surrender and allows former slave owners to start worming their way back into the Union using 'bonded servants' and 'hired help' forced to work for less than the price of food!"

I heard Samjack spit on the ground in anger.

"This war was about more than freeing the Coloreds. It was about abolishing it for everyone, forever. That's why we were called Abolitionists.

"We had it within our grasp, and he capitulated again. Not only that, but he tried to shut me down. Tried to hide all the work we had done, bury it under the rug to be forgotten. 'No one would understand,' he said. Well, I understood. I understood he was weak and would always bow to pressure. That's why I had him killed."

Mary tried to say something, but it sounded like they gagged her. I heard her put up a struggle, but it stopped with the sound of a soft thump. As soon as the metal box began to move, I realized I must be in one of the minecarts underneath the buildings. Samjack must have lied to me about not completing his underground rail system.

I was wheeled for quite some distance before the cart stopped and I was lifted out again. When my blindfold was removed, I found myself in a small earthen storm cellar. Samjack stood just outside the door, under an electric light, in what appeared to be one of the tunnels.

"I'm sorry it had to be this way," Captain Samjack genuinely seemed disappointed. "I had looked forward to working with you. You were a very talented man." He closed the door and the lock clicked with a sense of finality. My mind wouldn't let go of the way he had referred to me in the past tense.

I don't know how much time passed before I worked my hands free. I fumbled at my vest pocket and put my glasses back on. A futile gesture, I realized, but one I felt compelled to do nonetheless. In doing so I realized I still had tools shoved in my vest pockets from when I had been working at my workbench.

Ah, that seemed so long ago. If only I had stayed there a bit longer, or drank some water, anything to make this different.

I pushed the thoughts aside and took inventory as best I could, although I knew I had nothing very useful. A tiny file, a smaller pick, a few loose gears, and some thin wire. Then my hand landed upon the little flattened sphere.

My eyes went wide. How could I have forgotten? That was why I had quit working! I had completed the miniature perpetual motion engine.

I released the stop lever I had built into it, remembering the stroke of genius I'd had in a moment of delusion that had solved Samjack's problem of starting and stopping. I twisted the equatorial gear with a quick flick of the wrist and restarted the motor with a silent hum that shook in my hand.

The gyroscopic effect of the spinning gear made it difficult for me to rotate the motor, but within only a few minutes I had devised a way to attach my file to it and had a cutting machine.

I focused my attention on the lock bolt, as it would require the least amount of cutting to open the door, and within fifteen minutes I was able to break the bolt with a good kick to the door.

I stood in the tunnel exhilarated. I had escaped. But I had no idea what to do now. There were several other doors like the one I had just exited, but investigation revealed them to all be locked, and no sounds came from the other sides.

I shut off the motor, put it back in my pocket, and pushed on down the tunnel, picking a direction at random. I moved quickly, feeling exposed. The electric lights I had so enjoyed before now rendered the tunnels devoid of places to secret myself should anyone appear.

Eventually the tunnel opened up into the giant cavern Samjack had shown me. Peeking in, I saw men still working among the piles of stuff being stacked and stored. I could not follow the tracks past them and not be seen, but the far side of the cave still vanished into blackness where the lights did not shine.

I noticed the pipes running alongside the tracks here veered away into the darkness for some reason. I recalled pipes had run next to the tracks on the far side of the cavern, so they must meet back up, I reasoned. I could follow them in the dark, circle around on the far side where I would not be seen and make my escape when they rejoined the tracks.

I went slowly so my movement would not attract attention until I was sure I was lost in the darkness. It was easier to see than I thought it would be. Enough ambient light made its way out into the cave to allow me to see the gleam of the pipe in the dark.

I walked with my hands out in front of me so I wouldn't run into anything. A wise decision as the pipe soon led me into a small forest of stalagmites that reflected the light oddly, like mirrored surfaces.

I tripped on a smaller pipe branching off the main one. Looking closely, I saw the pipe split off to each of the metal pillars.

"Please…" the word hissed near my ear and I nearly fell down in terror.

"Please kill me." Breathy and barely audible, the words were distinct but distant, as though hidden behind a door.

I looked around frantically and discovered eyes looking at me, inches from my face. I swallowed hard and stepped backwards, bumping into another gleaming column. As I stared I started to be able to make out the shapes of men towering over me. Ten foot tall, metallic men- with human eyes peeking out from slots on their chests.

"Oh, dear god…" I murmured.

"There is no god here," a different voice, raspy and broken answered from my right. "You are in Hell."

Men in Samjack's blue uniforms hurried into the cavern shouting questions to those working in the lights. They were searching for me.

"You must hurry," Faber hissed at me. "They will search here soon."

"Hurry…" echoed Smythe weakly. "Please…"

I didn't answer. I set about to the task that had befallen me. The task of releasing these poor souls from Samjack's Hell.

I couldn't imagine what it must have been like to have been transformed into a clockwork man who was never wound up, and placed into storage in this black cave. I hurried past hundreds of them, all lined up in rows like toy soldiers.

When Smythe had sobbed the question of how long he had been trapped in here, I told him I didn't know. I hadn't the heart to tell him it had been a year. As a special punishment for being spies, neither Faber nor Smythe had undergone the 'mind numbing' procedure the others had— a trick Samjack had apparently learned after seeing soldiers with bullet wounds to the foreheads, Faber had said. It numbed the pain and made them compliant.

That must have been why Samjack's men had worn such stupefied expressions when capturing Mary and myself. They'd had their minds numbed.

I stepped over the little nutrient pipes coming off the main pipe to each tin man, carrying a solution to keep what was left of their bodies alive. Finally I found the place I had been told to look for. A huge fulcrum lever chained down to the ground so that it held a large gear wheel up and disengaged. I pulled out my new motorized pocket cutter and started in on the lock.

The cutting sound echoed through the cavern and soon the men stacking the metal parts of yet-to-be assembled human automatons were peering into the darkness towards me. Then they went back to work. I realized they must have had their brains numbed, too.

The lock gave way under my cutter and the gears fell into place with a grinding sound as the teeth fought each other to mesh. Lights flickered and came on above me, illuminating the entire cavern for the first time.

Hundreds of polished metal men stood in two straight lines, each with a rod connecting from the middle of their eight foot high back to the now spinning gears along the cave wall. They were clockwork men, all getting wound up at the same time.

The sound of shouting caught my attention over the hum of the gears, and I spied Samjack's men running into the cavern, pistols held high. One of them pointed at me and they all broke into a run towards me.

I froze. I didn't know what to do. There was nowhere to go in the open cavern. I was trapped in a giant room. I put my hands up in surrender.

"Disarm them." A strange mechanical voice filled the room and the three metal men nearest my accosters stepped forward with resounding metal clangs. The rods winding the springs in their backs pulled out easily and the nutrient pipes disengaged from their legs without spilling more than a few drops.

Samjack's men didn't have a chance. Giant metal hands ripped the guns out from their hands like toys taken from children. Two of the men fell to the floor clutching wounded hands, while the other three turned and ran back out into the tunnels.

The workers had stopped stacking the metal pieces and now stared.

I ran back towards Smythe and Faber. They had already disengaged from their keys. Smythe was walking in a huge clanking circle, crying and sobbing, a strange strangled mechanical noise. I decided Samjack's torture had broken him.

"Thank you." Faber spoke to me with a mechanical voice; it was a miniature Euphonia Talking Machine. "I will be forever grateful, although I can never repay you. Please, stand aside so you do not get hurt."

He stomped out to the front of all of the metal men and began to speak. "These are your orders: Destroy all of Captain Samjack's Emporium. Leave no building standing. Do not harm civilians. Kill any soldier who fires upon you. Go."

The metal men with the human eyes hidden behind their chests began pulling away from their tethers. Some marched straight across the cavern to the piles of crates and began smashing them. One began ripping up the minecart tracks; another attacked the gears spinning on the cavern wall.

As the lights began to flicker, the mesmerizing spell of the violence and destruction was broken, and I realized I needed to get out of the cavern.

I raced back into the tunnel I had been held captive in, as none of the metal men had yet gone that way. The sounds of destruction echoed behind me, and I could feel the shaking in the ground. As I hurried to make my escape, the sound of someone calling for help caught my attention.

It was Mary, calling from behind a locked door.

"Help! Help me!"

"Mary! It's me! Peter Henlein. I'm going to get you out." I pulled out my pocket cutter and started on her door.

When we reached the surface, pandemonium had already struck. People were running in droves for the stables on the outskirts of the grounds. Gaping holes had been torn into the sides of the hotels. Fires had broken out in several places.

The metal men were thorough. One stopped to pop each electric light as it went by them. Another had found the beautiful steam engine horse I had admired so, and was systematically dismembering it. It nearly broke my heart.

Mary was tugging at my arm. I turned to look where she was pointing.

Captain Samjack was doing battle with a metal man. He rolled quickly under the swipe of a giant hand and came up with his pistol drawn. He shoved it into the peephole in the automaton's chest and fired.

The clockwork/man hybrid spun out of control, losing balance and twitching all limbs in an uncontrolled and completely inhuman way. It fell to the ground, crushing a small tree as it went, and continued to jerk and convulse.

A giant explosion rocked the grounds, knocking everything human off their feet. I looked up to see one of the clockwork men and several large pieces of metal falling back to the ground.

"They must have ruptured one of the steam engines," I told Mary. "There will be more. We have to get out of here!"

We picked ourselves up and started to run with the rest of the fleeing guests. I saw Samjack kill another of his creations and stride on to the next, his black hair and moustache in disarray, but his pride and dignity shining through each step. He dropped two more metal giants with hardly a pause, but then was caught from behind by a giant hand.

I stopped running to watch, and Mary stopped beside me.

The metal man had grabbed Samjack around the middle with one hand and pulled his pistol away with the other. He brought Samjack's face close to the peep hole to get a good look at him. I heard the mechanical voice, although I could not make out the words, and knew it was Faber.

Samjack punched at the metal chest with strength beyond any mere human, denting it and rocking Faber backwards two steps. Holding the captain at arms' length Faber ripped of his shirt, exposing a metal framework covering Samjack's torso and giving him the extra strength.

Samjack kicked and punched at the big arm, but found no leverage, rendering his mechanical enhancements useless.

When Faber reached out with his other hand and grabbed Samjack's head, I looked away. Or at least I tell myself I did.

Mary screamed and we ran. We dodged tromping giant clockwork men, fleeing guests and flying pieces of metal as another steam engine exploded somewhere. The stables were full of panicked horses and people fighting each other over the steeds, so we pushed on until we broke free of the crowds.

I led Mary up a hill, avoiding the road and trampling horses. We wound our way through trees and brush until Mary stopped me and pointed back towards the battlefield.

As the sun began to set, we watched the fires flicker and the steam clouds billow out of the remains of Captain Samjack's twisted dream. A dream I had been enamored with until I had seen what lay beneath his fabricated and polished silver lining.

I don't know if Mary realized what was happening when one of the metal men turned on the others. I watched the firelight reflect off Faber's silver body as he began tracking down each of the other silver men and punching them repeatedly in the peephole in the chest. He was setting them free, I knew, but the tears ran down my face anyway.

As Mary buried her face in my shoulder, I heard her crying, too, and I wondered if Faber really had been her fiancée. As the metal man below smashed and fought, I wondered if she realized it was Faber.

*If the minority will not acquiesce, the majority must, or the Government must cease. There is no other alternative, for continuing the Government is acquiescence on one side or the other.*

—Abraham Lincoln
First Inaugural Address
Monday, March 4, 1861

# A BETTER PLACE TO DIE

The steady *chunk-chunk-chunk* sound of Mighty Miner, mechanically digging its way deeper into the side of the mountain, lulled Whip as he sat next to the campfire, nearly fifty yards away. There was a slight chill in the night air, and Whip reckoned he would need to get around to building a shelter soon, if he was going to winter here. Sleeping in the mine during a rain was fine, but the thought of getting snowed up inside the dark hole wasn't a pleasant one.

Since being freed, Whip had been steadily making his way west, taking what jobs he could find. It had taken him four years to get to the New Mexico Territories and, in all that time, he'd only seen snow once, but once was enough to know winter was going to be hard in this country.

A wind picked up and rushed through the needles of the pine trees, sounding like a rushing river. Whip smiled at the sound. While there had been pine trees in Louisiana, they hadn't sounded like this in the wind. It was a lonesome sound, one that echoed the feeling of the enormous open world around him, yet one that gave him a peaceful feeling about being out in the great big world.

Embers stirred from the fire and swirled up into the night sky, their bright orange a warm contrast to the cool white of the stars.

This was a better place to die than the plantation he'd been born into, newfound freedom or not. His grandfather would have loved this strange, dry land with its ruddy, barren mountains. There wasn't a bayou close enough for most folk around here to even know the word. Whip himself was more partial to the greener parts of this country, especially the pine forests, but he didn't miss the red bugs or leeches one whit.

As he fought off sleep, Whip's head jerked up, pulling his chin up off his chest. He shook off memories of dead family and friends and places he'd never see again. Stretching and yawning, he decided there wasn't any reason to put off sleep anymore.

"Come on, Mighty Miner!" he called as he stood up and limped off the pain in his joints. "It's tha' time o' night."

Radiant light, from the fire under Mighty Miner's boiler, made the mouth of the mineshaft glow warmly, and Whip had no problems finding his way toward it in the dark night. The acrid smell of smoke and the dank of settling steam washed over Whip as he entered the warm tunnel. The rhythmic *chunk-chunk-chunk* grew loud and ear-pounding in the confined space.

Built onto a mine cart, and using a boiler and mechanics similar to a railroad engine, Mighty Miner worked hard at tunneling into the mountainside. With six pneumatic pick axes swinging at the rock in alternating time, it worked faster, harder, and longer than any six men could, and it did so in a smaller area without worry of the men hitting each other.

Sheet metal catchers, positioned below the axes, collected falling debris as the picks worked their way up and down the rock face in a sweeping motion. The same piston driving the axes lifted the catchers up as the tools worked upwards, dumping the rocks and ore into the mine cart.

"I guess we called it a night just in time!" Whip said, reaching the machine and seeing the mine cart was nearly full. He affectionately patted the side of the slightly rusted cart, making a solid thumping sound, and moved on to the controls.

Easing back levers, Whip sighed with relief as the pick axes slowed and the sound of iron striking stone faded, leaving a ringing in his ears. Whip pulled another lever and, in a hiss of steam, the axes and catchers folded up tight against the body of Might Miner, dropping the last of the rocks into the cart.

"Okay, son, let's get outta here." Whip slowly turned a crank and Mighty Miner began chuffing like a small train and moving backward up the mineshaft on metal train wheels adapted with spikes and blades welded on for traction.

Whip walked alongside the machine, controlling the speed and gently correcting course up the short mineshaft. After only a week, Mighty Miner had tunneled nearly ten yards into the hard rock mountainside.

"We gonna get you unloaded and over by the fire so's I can see, and then we'll get you taken care of," Whip told the machine as they exited the mine. He steered it over to an embankment and pulled another lever to dump the contents of the mine cart onto a growing pile of tailings. "I'll sort through this in the daylight on the morrow, see if we've found any of them golden fingers in that rock yet."

Mighty Miner groaned as something prevented the cart from settling back into place.

"Sounds like you got a rock in yor shoe. Don' worry. I'll see to that, too." Whip turned the crank and lead Mighty Miner to the campfire as the machine chuffed steam out around his ankles.

When the machine was parked in front of the fire, Whip released the steam valve in a loud hiss that near guaranteed safety from predators for the rest of the night. He opened the fire grate and carefully shoveled the still burning coals out and onto his own fire, and then he cleaned out the ash pan. "You et good today! I'm 'a need to cut you more wood."

As the boiler cooled, popping and ticking quietly in the night, Whip set about oiling and greasing everything from the controls to the wheel bearings. "Yesser. An ounce a prevention," he told the machine. "'Sides, I knows you like it. Everyone like a good rubdown after a hard day's work, and I never knowed nobody what worked harder 'n you. Now, let's see about that rock…"

Whip grabbed a long switch and lit one end in the campfire. Using the small flame to see, he stuck the twig into the crevasses around the mine cart until he spotted the offending rock. "There he is! Don' worry, I'll have him out in no time."

He dug at the rock with a bigger stick until he worked it out, then he held it up for Mighty Miner to see. "There's the fella what was stuck in yor craw!"

Firelight glinted off the rock and Whip looked closer.

"Well lookee that! He's a goldie!"

Steam hissed, signaling Mighty Miner was up to pressure and ready to work.

"And a good morning to you!" Whip said. "You a bit of a slow riser this morning. Guess you didn't like that water I spilled in yor firepan. Sorry 'bout that. I'm startin' to get shaky w' age, and the crick was awful cold this morn! But yor boiler is good full an' I got lots a fresh wood for you."

The rising sun broke through the tree line and lit the small camp with scattered beams of light, setting the puffing steam clouds aglow as they drifted away from the machine.

"There's the sun! 'Bout time he got here. I been waitin' so's I can get a good look at what you was doin' down in that hole." Whip patted the machine, making a hollow thumping sound, and hurried over his gear. "Sunlight works a lot better'n candles," he said as he pulled two mirrors out. One was the size of a dinner plate, and the other was a small hand mirror.

Whip sat the larger of the two in front of the shaft, using rocks to hold it in place and a cloth to protect it from scratches. He adjusted the mirror until it reflected a beam of light down into the shaft and lit up the back rock face. Standing up, he took a moment and admired the mirror. It was a fine piece of craftsmanship. Better than any he'd ever seen in the Master's house.

Whip's face clouded at the thought.

Mighty Miner whistled as steam vented under a slow pressure release.

"You're right, as usual," Whip said, dismissing the thought. He took a deep breath and faced into the sun, eyes closed, feeling the warmth. Some things could never be forgotten, but that didn't mean they needed to be dwelt on.

Whip hurried back to the machine and adjusted the valves to relieve the steam pressure. He'd have about a quarter hour before Mighty Miner would get impatient again.

Hurrying down into the mine, Whip watched his shadow

shrink in front of him as he moved forward in the mirror's beam of light. At the end of the shaft he held out the smaller mirror, putting it in the beam to reflect the light around the tunnel.

Examining the work Mighty Miner had done the day before, he mused aloud. "Where did that lil' goldie fella come from…"

The reflected spot of light traveled across the wall, revealing dull colored stone, as he turned his hand. A hint of white, near the rounded corner of the end of the tunnel, caught Whip's eye, and he turned the mirror to light it up.

"There you are," he whispered, recognizing the quartz vein as a place where gold could be found.

He stepped closer and lost his light. Feeling foolish, he stepped backward to recapture the beam of light with his mirror, but the tunnel had gone dark. He looked back up the shaft and saw a figure standing between him and the larger mirror.

"There he is!" A man's voice echoed down into the shaft. The figure moved, exposing the mirror and sending the beam back down, blinding Whip as he looked straight into it.

Whip put his hand up to block the light and vaguely made out the figure standing next to the mirror. Before Whip could say anything, a second figure appeared. The pistol in the man's hand, silhouetted in the light, was very clear.

"Come on out, boy!" the second man called.

Whip clenched his jaw. Some part of him, deep down, had known he'd be called that again, but he'd still allowed himself to believe he could get far enough west to get away from it. The shattering of the dream hurt more than the word itself.

Keeping his hands where they could easily be seen, Whip came out of the mineshaft and into the daylight. The man with the pistol wasn't directly pointing it at him, so Whip felt that was a good sign, but the other man's hand rested on his own holstered weapon, showing he was ready to draw it at any time.

"No sign of the old man, Wallace," a third voice called from Whip's left.

Whip turned to see another man on horseback.

"No horses, neither," the man said. "Maybe the old man took them and went into town?"

"Mr. Sparrow's dead," Whip said, careful not to make any threatening moves. "He passed on near a month ago. Bit by a rattler."

Mighty Miner began whispering steam as the boiler reached pressure again.

"That the contraption, Ronald?" The man with the gun pointed at Mighty Miner. The man made Whip nervous. Not just because he held the gun, but because he had the same cruel eyes Whip had seen in so many white men.

"Yep," answered the man standing next to the mirror. He was young, and looked familiar, but Whip couldn't place him. "Just like I told you, Wallace, that thing can out-dig any ten men."

The puffing of the steam increased as the machine's internal pressure rose.

The third man dismounted, dropping his horse's reins to the ground next to the other men's two horses, and approached Mighty Miner. "If Sparrow's dead, why you out here with his machine?" he asked without looking at Whip.

"He give it t' me, with his dyin' breath."

The other two men exchanged glances. "Where's his horses?" Wallace asked, still holding the pistol half raised.

"I took 'em to town an' traded them for supplies and rights to this land."

Mighty Miner's pressure increased to a near steady hiss, rising in pitch, and the man standing next to it began examining the controls.

"Ha! Hear that?" Ronald's laugh was mirthless. "He moves in here and takes my job, now he thinks he can have the land, too!"

The young man's comment nudged Whip's memory, and he finally recognized him. Mr. Sparrow had hired Whip at ten dollars a month, plus food and a bit stake in anything they found. Ronald had demanded for Mr. Sparrow to hire him instead, but for two dollars a day and half share of any findings. Mr. Sparrow had laughed in the young man's face and walked away. There had been a lot of cursing about paying a slave to do a real man's job aimed at his back, but Mr. Sparrow had just walked away.

Whip hadn't thought much about any more about the exchange. It wasn't much different than most interactions he'd had since the war.

"I can't hear nothin' over that infernal noise! Springer! Shut that damned thing down!" The man with the pistol hollered to the man standing next to Mighty Miner.

With a turn of a gear, Springer shut off the steam.

"Be careful," Whip called out, "or you'll hurt 'im!"

"I don't think slaves are allowed to own property," Ronald sneered. The hand on his holster was no longer relaxed. "Especially escaped slaves."

"He ain't no slave." Wallace had a mocking tone in his voice. "He's a *freed man*!"

An angry hissing sound came from Mighty Miner, growing louder by the second.

"You need to take care of him," Whip warned Springer, pointing at Mighty Miner.

"He's a slave. I know it," said Ronald, ignoring Whip's warning. "Look at the whip scar across his face. Only slaves get marked like that. Pretty sure it means he's done run away before!"

Whip felt the scar across his left cheek burn as it was mentioned. He'd gotten it as a boy by being foolish enough to look over his shoulder to see when the Master was going to start whipping him. It had not only scarred him, it had named him.

"Naw," Wallace waved his pistol as he talked. "He's *free* now. *Free* to go where he wants, *free* to do what he wants… and *free* of anyone who values his sorry hide."

"You mean, he's *free* to die?" Ronald drew his pistol in an unhurried move.

Mighty Miner groaned and the escaping steam began to scream.

"Mister," Whip pointed at the man next to Mighty Miner, "if you don't relieve that pressure, he's gonna blow!"

A pistol fired and Whip felt a hot punch to his gut. He looked down to see wet red spreading down his worn and dirty cotton shirt. Stumbling back a step, Whip dropped the hand mirror. It shattered on a rock, the shards sending reflections of golden morning sunlight scattering across the faces of the men, the machine, and the mine.

Ronald, holding a smoking pistol, laughed. "You see the look on his face? He didn't even see it comin'!"

A second shot rang out and the laughter stopped. Ronald dropped his pistol and turned sideways, showing Whip the hole in the side of his head before he fell to the ground.

"Jesus Christ!" Wallace whirled toward Mighty Miner, his gun searching for a target.

"It blew a rivet!" Springer looked stunned.

"Shut the damned thing off before it blows more!"

Frantically grabbing at controls, Springer sent the axes and catchers flailing at a raging speed.

*Chunk-chunk-chunk!*

The sudden jerk of motion shook Mighty Miner, rocking it sideways. The horses reared and bolted at the sight of the flailing metal creature waving six arms at them. Shuddering and tipping precariously to one side, Mighty Miner came crashing back down upon Springer's foot with a spiked steel wheel.

*Chunk-chunk-chunk!*

Springer screamed and fell, foot trapped under the thrashing machine. "Help me!" He tried to reach the controls but fell short. "Help!"

*Chunk-chunk-chunk!*

An axe head, swinging too hard and too fast without ever meeting resistance, snapped free of its handle and spun off, up into the air, higher than the tree tops. The change in balance rocked the machine again, and it bounced, releasing Springer's foot, but then came crashing back down upon it again, and again, piston-like. The rocking motion worked the machine sideways, walking it toward Springer by fractions of an inch with each landing, crushing more of his foot each time it landed.

*Chunk-chunk-chunk!*

Wallace ran to help just as Springer's desperate swipe at the controls haphazardly hit the gears and cranks, setting Mighty Miner lurching forward at a speed it was never meant to travel. The off-balance machine plowed right into the charging Wallace. An upward swinging pick gutted him, a downward one, through his skull, silenced his scream.

*Chunk-chunk-chunk!*

Wallace's body was shredded and sprayed across the campsite in an instant as Mighty Miner, moving at uncontrolled speed, roared forward, off-kilter on two side wheels. Travelling in a tight circle, it came back to Springer, who seemed unable to remove his damaged foot from the hole in the ground it had been pressed into. Springer screamed as the machine bore down upon him.

*Chunk-chunk-chunk!*

Whip, looked away, unable to watch the man die, and was surprised to find himself kneeling on the ground. He hadn't remembered falling to his knees. The mirror shards on the ground around him sparkled with perfect reflections of the clear blue sky.

The sound of a curious bird's inquisitive chirp caught Whip's attention, and he looked up.

His little camp was silent.

Mighty Miner was stopped, mere feet away from Whip. The only sign of life left in its boiler was small steam trail, whisping up, aspiring to become one of the high, thin clouds. A few smoking pieces of wood were spread across the ground and Whip wasn't sure if they had been scattered from the campfire or dumped from Mighty Miner's open fire grill.

As he stared at the machine, he spotted the place where the rivet had blown, leaving a bulging spot on Mighty Miner's belly.

Whip tried to stand, but hot pain kept him on his knees. Using one hand to press the heat back into his own belly, he made a limping, three-limbed crawl to Mighty Miner's side.

He patted the side of the machine, ignoring the heat of the metal on his hand, and then dropped to a sitting position, leaning back against a wheel covered in reddish mud.

"You done good, son," Whip whispered. "I wish you hadn't hurt yorself like tha', but you done good."

He looked up to the sun, still nowhere near midday height, and forced his scowl into a grin.

"Lots o' ways I thought I'd go over th' years," he said. "Next to a frien' like you, both o' us gutshot, warn't never one of 'em."

Mighty Miner creaked and popped as it cooled.

"Well, if we gots to, we gots to," Whip said. "An' this a better place to die than most I seen."

*Chunk-chunk-chunk!*

The sound lulled Whip as he slept.

*Chunk-chunk-chunk!*

He furrowed his brows in confusion and opened his eyes. The room was bright with open curtains and windows letting the sun in.

*Chunk-chunk-chunk!*

Whip tried to sit up, but a deep, sharp pinching pain in his side stopped him and he moaned in surprise, gently laying himself back onto the softest bed he'd ever slept on.

*Chunk-chunk-chunk!*

A woman came in, carrying a mug. "I thought I heard you!" She smiled at him. "Here. Doc says you need to drink this. But drink it slow, and only a little at a time, so that it stays down."

Whip hesitated to take the mug. No white woman had ever handed him something, except to give him an errand or a chore to do. Certainly never something in a manner that indicated she was serving him.

*Chunk-chunk-chunk!*

"Go on, take it," she encouraged.

Whip took it with a shaky hand. "Wha's that sound?" he asked, wishing he could see more than just blue sky out the window.

*Chunk-chunk-chunk!*

"Smithy has got your machine back up and running good as new, sounds like," she answered. "He's been working on it all week." She lowered her voice. "The mayor told him to fix it, but I'm sure he would have done it anyway. He was terribly fascinated by how it works."

"Mayor?" Whip asked.

"Yup," a man said, walking into the room. He wore a badge on the front of his shirt. "The mayor is convinced we're gonna have a gold rush, now that you've hit pay. Figures this little town is gonna grow big and fast."

Whip looked back and forth between the man and the

woman, confused.

"When those boys' horses came wondering back into town, I went lookin' to see what happened," the man told him. "I figured Indians. Imagine my surprise to find they'd tried to jump your claim. And that they'd killed themselves trying to figure out your machine."

Whip tried to sit up again, and was again stopped by the pain.

The man reached into his pocket and pulled out a nugget the size of a walnut, holding it up for Whip to see. "Hope you don't mind. We took a little to cover the expense of doctorin' you up and repairing your machine. You understand."

Whip sunk back into the soft bed and closed his eyes.

"We need to let him rest," the woman whispered.

Whip smiled. This would be a good place to die. But not yet. Meanwhile, he had a friend to check in on.

*Chunk-chunk-chunk!*

The bullet hit Despo right between the eyes.

Bouncing off his forehead, it landed in the dirt, inches from his nose. Despo, buried up to his neck in the sandy soil of a dry riverbed, turned his eyes up from the unfired .44 round to the handlebar-mustachioed outlaw towering over him.

The outlaw grinned, revealing spotted, wide-spaced teeth. "I understand it's proper et-i-kate to leave a man with a last bullet. Don't say I never gave you nothin', *Despo*." Frenchie drew the name out, filling it with disgust as he looked down. The five men standing behind him barked laughter like hyenas at a kill. "What kind of stupid name is that anyway? *Des-po*? Figure yerself a desperado or somethin'? Not really a fitting name for a lawman, is it?"

Ignoring the comment, Despo looked back to the .44 slug lying inches from his nose. "That'd be a lot more helpful if you'd give back my gun as well," he said.

"Shit." Marcus Hamby stepped forward and lightly punched Frenchie in the arm. "Give the man an inch and he wants a goddamn mile!"

Laughter erupted again.

"Well, it don't hurt none to ask, I guess." Frenchie gave a melodramatic shrug. Then he pulled his foot back and kicked Despo in the face.

White pain flashed in Despo's vision, blinding him and taking his breath away.

"Nope. I was wrong. Looks like it did hurt to ask." More laughter.

Marcus leaned over, hands on his knees, and looked Despo in the face. "Damn, boy. I do believe you've got a broken nose.

Didn't your momma warn you that's what happens when you stick it places it don't belong?" He stood up and turned away from the interred man, nonchalantly looking at the sun.

"Gettin' mighty warm," Marcus said. "I think it's gonna be a hot one today." He turned to Frenchie. "What say we head down to the swimmin' hole? Seems like a good day to try to keep cool."

"That sounds like a good idea. Maybe we'll go fishin'. All right boys, let's go cool off!" Frenchie said.

The men gave a cheer and gathered up the shovels they had used to dig the five-foot vertical hole now holding Despo. When they were packed, the outlaws mounted, lined up, and took turns riding their horses over the small mound of dirt they had planted Despo in.

An explosion of hooves flashed past Despo's face, some clipping his ears and his broken nose. When the flurry stopped, Despo opened his eyes to find Frenchie looking down at him from astride his horse. He had Despo's own horse tethered on a lead, spoils claimed by the victor.

"Next time," Frenchie said, "maybe you'll think twice about whether or not you want to be such a hothead." He looked up at the sun and grinned before running his horse at Despo's head.

Despo awoke unable to see and gasping for air. Pain pounded in his head. Being encased in earth limited his breath, and his nose was swollen shut. He couldn't even cough the dust out of his lungs. Panicking, his struggles nearly caused him to pass out again, and he was forced to calm.

The sun overhead made his dark hair feel like someone had built a campfire in it.

Blinking to break his blood-encrusted eyelids free, he noted the dried blood in the sand in front of his face. Frenchie's horse apparently hadn't stepped around him.

His eyes focused on the brass casing of the.44 bullet lying in front of him. The horses' hooves had knocked it unbearably close. He could almost touch it with his tongue.

Almost.

It was a good final taunt, and he'd have tipped his hat to Frenchie for it, if Frenchie hadn't stolen his hat, too.

Fingers, toes, hands, feet…everything was numb. He couldn't feel or move any of them. His whole body was a dull, disconnected ache. It was easy to imagine he didn't even have a body, that he was just a head lying on the ground in the middle of the Arizona desert.

He tried to swallow, but his mouth was too dry.

In the distance, a bird circled against the blue sky.

It was peaceful, in its own way, and Despo found it wasn't so bad, other than the fire on top of his head.

He wondered how long it would take for the fire to burn down through his skull, into his brain, and make him go mad.

"I'm disappointed." A woman's voice, rich and sweet, spoke from behind him.

The voice didn't disturb his newfound calm. Despo twisted his head to see anyway. He saw nothing. "Hello?" His voice creaked like a leather hinge.

"You had so much potential…Despo." Her voice sounded familiar, but he couldn't place it.

"Who's there?"

"I approve of the name you took. It's fitting."

Despo searched his memory for a woman who would know Despo was not his real name, but found none. Only his dead family could have known.

"I suppose I should praise you for what you managed to accomplish, rather than point out the failings of your ending."

"Who are you?"

"You have been a good protector of the innocent. Seems you have a gift for it. Thirty-two men brought to justice. Twenty-eight of them singlehandedly."

Despo gave up trying to see. Either the woman would reveal herself or she wouldn't. There was nothing to do about it.

"What made you decide you could just ride into Frenchie's camp and take on his whole gang?"

"They were all drunk," Despo muttered. He worked his tongue around inside his mouth, trying to make enough spit to continue talking, but there was no moisture left.

"They are always drunk. It is not a condition that impairs the abilities valuable to men like them."

Despo didn't respond. There was no woman behind him. There couldn't be. The fire had burned down into his brain without him knowing it. He had gone insane.

The bird circling in the distant sky grew larger as it lazily worked its way closer. Soon he could make out the naked red head of the turkey vulture; then, before he realized how close it was coming, it was already landing in front of him.

The bird cocked a beady eye at him, its pale eyelid flashing blue as it blinked. It hopped closer, waiting for his reaction.

Immobilized, unable to take a deep breath, and with a dry, swollen tongue, Despo couldn't even spit at the carrion eater.

It hopped up, landing on his head, and Despo winced as talons dug into his skull, pressing the fire-hot hair down against his skull and cooking his brain even more.

Squeezing his dry eyes shut, he waited for the beak to pierce his eyelids and peck the eyeballs from his skull.

The weight on his head shifted as the vulture tried to keep its balance, but the striking blow never came. Gradually, Despo opened his eyes and found his head in the shadow of the bird's outstretched wings.

"She'll stay for a little while," the woman's voice came from behind Despo again. "The day is hot for her, too, and absorbing sun will heat her up quickly."

"Wha—?" Despo tried to speak but his throat was nearly swollen shut from lack of moisture.

"I have watched you for many years, Despo. Since before you were born. Consider this a final courtesy, out of respect for your mother."

Terrible images flashed through his mind. Horses and people screaming and running. His mother had been murdered when he was very young. His mother, his family, his entire village— massacred.

"She was a good woman. Respectful. Kind. Nurturing," the woman said.

50

His mother had been a *curandera*, a witch, a healer. She had never hurt anyone. She hadn't deserved to die like that.

"I was the one who cast the spell of silence upon you," the woman continued.

As far as Despo knew, he was the only survivor. The only one, out of a village of a hundred, not chased down and clubbed or beaten or raped to death. He had been playing in his favorite place: a cool green thicket of cactus, where his small body could crawl back in between the spines and oversized leaves of the giant agave, where the older kids couldn't reach him.

When the attack on his village came, he found himself trapped inside, unable to find his way back out of the prickly maze. His voice had frozen, refusing to allow him to call out. As night fell, and the bandits left, he had finally found his way back out and wandered into what was left of his village. There were no survivors. It had been rendered *despoblado*—a ghost town.

"Your mother's final wish was that I watch over you. I have done what I could throughout the years. It was my final gift to her. But there are limits to what even I can do. Men have a will of their own, and they don't often stop to listen to my suggestions."

"Do you have any suggestions for me now?" Despo croaked out harsh, broken words, but the woman seemed to understand them.

"Your family is gone. The men who killed them are gone as well. Dead years ago. Every last one. You have nothing left to prove. You never did. You just didn't realize it." The woman's voice seemed to whisper in his ear. "Life is a gift. Everything, everything all around us is a gift. Gifts are to be enjoyed. Gifts are to be used. Use your gifts wisely."

A dry breeze ruffled his hair, unbalancing the buzzard on his head, and he knew the woman was gone.

The bird jumped down awkwardly, wings and talons scraping up sand as it righted itself. With a pump of its wings, the turkey vulture leapt into the sky, swirling dust into Despo's eyes.

Something hot hit under his chin. Trying to blink the dust away, Despo tilted his head and lifted his jaw, trying to prevent it from touching the hot thing. It stuck to the sweat on his skin at first, then dropped off and rolled out from under his chin. Cocking his head sideways, he looked down at it with one eye.

It was the bullet.

Shining brightly in the hot sun, it was so close Despo could smell the heated brass casing.

He couldn't stop staring at the inch of polished brass with the quarter inch of dull lead on top. He turned his head from side to side, switching eyes until they ached worse than any pain he could remember. The whole world contracted into a tiny space he could hardly see, right in front of his face. He couldn't stop staring at it.

Out of desperation for the pain in his eyes, and his own sanity, he stuck out his tongue and tried to flip the damned thing away.

The hot metal stuck to his desiccated tongue and the bullet was pulled into his mouth, surprising and choking Despo. He caught the shell between his teeth and ripped it off the skin, moaning curses he couldn't voice and keeping his cracked lips spread wide so they wouldn't touch the blistering hot brass.

If only Frenchie were here, he'd get a belly laugh at the extra misery it had caused Despo.

The thought didn't anger Despo. Instead, he still felt the calm that had settled over him while watching the soaring bird riding the heat waves. The bird was back up there again, circling, and Despo wondered if it landing on his head had been a dream.

The woman's voice must have been a hallucination, and perhaps the bird had been too, but he held the bullet in his teeth. That much was real.

The calmness he felt in his soul was a gift. Was that proof the woman had been here, too?

He choked out a broken laugh, his lips still held wide around the bullet between his front teeth, as he felt the return of the fire on the top of his skull.

So many wonderful gifts today. Staring at the pale blue sky, he wondered how he could possibly put any of them to good use.

Despo rotated the inch-long bullet in his mouth, nearly dropping it. He panicked and bent his head forward, sticking the metal down into the dirt, trying not to lose it. It was the only gift he had received he could actually touch. He couldn't bear the thought of dropping it.

When he had a firm grip on it again, he lifted his head back up and stared down into the indentation in the soft sand he had made with it. Pushing the bullet as far forward in his teeth as he could, he began using sweeping motions back and forth, moving the sandy earth away from the front of his face.

Caked chunks, small bricks made from his own dried blood, cracked away and piled up. As he created a small furrow, he found it made room for him to rock his neck forward and back. Not much, but a little. The bullet was a poor digging tool, but it moved dirt, so he kept using it.

The more Despo wriggled his head around, the more the dirt around him seemed to move away from his throat, and he almost felt like he could breathe again.

When he reached the point that he had moved all the dirt he could with the bullet and his limited head motion, he pulled the dusty bullet all the way into his mouth and tucked it into his cheek. Even if he couldn't use it anymore, he was afraid to drop it lest he not be able to pick it up again.

His teeth, jaw, neck, and eyes ached, the pain giving his otherwise numb body some sense of life. The sun still shone down hotly, and he realized he wasn't even sweating anymore.

He was going to die soon.

He wished it would rain. Maybe just one more time before he died.

Exhaustion overtook him, and he slept.

The first drop of rain hit the top of Despo's head like a ball peen hammer, shocking him awake. Puffs of dust appeared in front of his face as giant beads of water slammed into the ground, leaving craters in the sand. An ice-cold drop hit his forehead and trickled into his eye, the moisture causing unbearable burning pain in the dry orb.

Trying to tilt his head back enough to catch a drop of rain in his mouth, he shifted the bullet tucked away in his cheek, tearing it away from the skin and leaving another raw spot inside his already ruined mouth. The first drop to make it into his mouth was the best and worst thing that had ever happened to him.

The moisture awakened every nerve ending in his body, and he screamed hoarsely as the pain increased in intensity as the rain began to come down in earnest.

Water pooled in the shallow impression below his chin, and as he wiggled his head, it made squelching sounds around his throat. He could feel the water sucking into, and shooting out of, the hole around his neck. As the rain picked up, he desperately used the puddling water to try to free himself.

His mouth burned as the moisture filled the cracks in his lips and tongue. The bullet clicked against his teeth as he tried to lick more off his dripping face. After what seemed like hours, Despo had managed to use the suction of the water seeping in around his body to be able to move his chest and shoulders back and forth, just a little.

Lightning flashed across the sky, and a thunderpeal chased it through the dark storm clouds. Rainwater pooled deep enough he had to keep his head tilted back to keep it out of his mouth, and he began to curse it as much as he had wished for it.

Struggling to loosen the mud around him, he became aware of a distant, growing rumble. Something he felt vibrating through his body. Stampede was the first thing Despo thought of. Then he realized he was in the middle of a dry riverbed. In a thunderstorm.

The crashing wave of water was upon him so quickly he hardly had a chance to hold his breath. Churning with mud and silt, the water smashed his head forward, threatening to snap his neck. In a heartbeat, his face was submerged, the rushing flood of rainwater tearing and pulling at his head. He fought to move, struggling not to lose his lungful of air in the onslaught. Water swirled around his head, digging at the loose soil he was buried in, making eddies that tore around him, sucking the dirt away.

Bent forward, face held to the sand by the force of the current, Despo felt the water digging down behind his back.

Writhing with fear and desperation, he managed to bend an elbow, then wiggle his arm, and finally rip his hand up and free from the sand. Clawing with the free hand, he began convulsing from lack of air. He clenched the bullet tightly in his teeth so he wouldn't open his mouth and let the water in.

Something hit him from behind and he reflexively caught at it. Branches, pulled downriver by the flood, tore at his fingers. He held tight as the water tugged on the tree and swirled around his body. When his other arm came free, he grabbed hold with both hands.

His lungs convulsed again, and again, fighting his sealed lips as the maelstrom roared around him. Finally, he no longer had say in what his body did, and his lips opened.

The water rushed in.

Despo woke shivering. Starlight set a stark contrast between the white sands and rocks of the desert and the black pool of water he lay in. His body ached and nearly refused when he tried to sit up, his shoulder and back too stiff and painful to move.

It took several minutes to roll over and crawl out of the puddle. His stomach heaved and he vomited water. The dark stain it left on the sand contained a glittering object.

The bullet Frenchie had left for him.

No longer a perfect cylinder, it showed dents from Despo's teeth.

A wild grin spread across Despo's face, breaking open the fissures in his lips. Blood filled his mouth as his weak, choked laughter carried out into the silence of the desert night.

"Ho-lee shit! Despo? Izzat really you?" Frenchie stood up from the Faro table, knocking over his bottle of whiskey as he slurred and stumbled to his feet. The slopping amber liquid soaked the cards and the money on the table, but the outlaw didn't notice.

As the patrons of the saloon stopped talking to see what the commotion was, three other men stood up, following Frenchie's lead.

"Sumbitch! It is!" Marcus Hamby stepped forward, letting go of the girl on his arm. "I'd recognize that busted nose anywhere." Laughter broke out from a couple places in the smoky den.

Frenchie, squinting bloodshot eyes at Despo, took a step towards him, his face unsmiling.

"Cain't be."

"It is." Despo's voice was as cracked as the healing blisters on his face.

When he was close enough to be sure he was really looking at Despo, Frenchie stopped and dropped his hand to his holster. "What do you want?"

Despo matched Frenchie's motion. "I realized I never properly thanked you for the parting gift you gave me. I just came here to put that right."

The silence in the saloon was broken by Frenchie's laughter. "You came here to use that bullet on me?" He turned to take in his men scattered among the other patrons around the room. "The bullet I gave you?" he said for them all to hear. "Out of the goodness of my heart?"

"No." Despo held out a hand. The dented .44 round rested in his palm. "I've already fired my last shot. I don't need it anymore. I came here to give it back to you. As a gift."

Frenchie didn't take his eyes off Despo's to look at the offering.

Despo turned his hand over, waiting for Frenchie to reach out, so he could drop it into the outlaw's hand.

"What game you playin' at?" Frenchie's voice lost its mirth as he glanced around the room. "You got lawmen here, watchin' me? Waiting to shoot as soon as I pull on you? You tryin' to bait me?" He turned and put his back to Despo. "It won't work! I don't draw on men for no reason, you hear me?" Frenchie raised his voice for the whole saloon to hear.

When no one answered, he slowly turned back to Despo and finally let his eyes drop to the bullet still being offered.

"I ain't gonna take it."

Despo shrugged and sat it on the Faro table next to the spilled liquor and Frenchie's scattered stake money. "It's there if you want it."

"Why would I? You think I'm a gonna carry it around and think about the day you didn't die?"

"Maybe."

"Why?"

"You gave me a gift. It changed my life. I'm a different person now. I'm giving you the gift back. Maybe it'll make you a different person, too."

"Different how, lawman?" Frenchie sneered disgustedly. "You look a mite sunburned, but that's about it. You're still the same idjut I buried up to his neck in the desert."

Someone in the back chortled.

Despo nodded. "I'd lay my badge down right here, to show you I'm not the same person I was, but…well, I don't know what you did with it."

"I know where it is!" Marcus Hamby called out. "And I gotta say, I know a couple of ladies who've been thrilled to find it there!"

Sporadic laughter broke out but faded quickly as Frenchie's hand moved back to the gun on his hip. "So, you're finally talking a language I understand. You don't need to hide behind the badge to take me down. I can respect that."

Shaking his head, Despo responded. "No. I didn't come here to fight you. I just came to offer a suggestion."

Frenchie laughed. "Lots a men given me suggestions on where ta go and what to do! Don't know that I've cared much to listen."

"Your choice. But I'll offer it nonetheless. Life is a gift. Everything is a gift. Enjoy your gifts and use them wisely. Gifts are meant to be enjoyed."

Despo turned and began walking out of the saloon.

"Wait!" Frenchie called out. "That's it? What kind of bullshit is that?"

"A suggestion," Despo responded over his shoulder. "Just a suggestion."

"I shoulda just shot you in the head when you was buried up to yer neck." Frenchie drew his gun. Three shots rang out.

Despo turned to see the outlaw fall, his men drawing their guns and rushing forward.

More shots. More men fell.

Despo shook his head sadly as three marshals came out of hiding and rounded up the men still breathing. He looked down at the blood dripping off the drooping mustache of the outlaw, not sure how he felt about the man's choice.

The woman in the desert had been right.

Men rarely listen to suggestions.

# New Mexico

# 1902

The rumble vibrating through the water in my bowl soothed me, and I dreamed of when I lived in open water, subject to the random currents caused by wind and temperature changes. I thought it was thunderstorms off in the distance. We'd had a lot lately and last night was one of the worst ever.

Johnathon, my human, hadn't yet opened the fancy lace curtains veiling our picture window to Main Street, so I continued to doze, slowly fluttering my fins, enjoying the lazy morning. All of the humans went to church Sunday mornings, including Johnathon, so Sundays were our little pawnshop's quietest mornings. We were closed for business, out of respect, Johnathon told me, but we often hosted the Sunday Luncheons. Everyone loved to look at Johnathon's collection of mysterious trinkets. And to come see me.

Shadows moving rapidly back and forth across the curtains roused me from my dream. The humans in our little town didn't usually hurry around so quickly. I heard shouting, which surprised me. I didn't often hear the sounds humans made outside of the immediate room my bowl was in. Walls tended to muffle all but the deepest and loudest noises.

Like the growing rumble.

As the shadows raced by, I found myself swimming in nervous circles. I don't usually feel restricted by my inability to swim through the air, and I haven't often regretted my decision to live above the surface with Johnathon, but as more humans shouted and ran by, I began to feel trapped in my bowl.

The alarm bell at the General Store clanged, and I knew something was wrong. Since the new church bell arrived, the old iron one was only used in emergencies.

I tried to relieve my anxiety by swimming quickly. I hurried back and forth in a straight line, instead of my usual circles, so I could keep an eye facing the window each time I turned. I knew Johnathon would come for me soon.

The alarm bell stopped, but the strange rumbling noise had grown disconcertingly loud, and the humans' shouting, though still desperate and fevered, began to fade. They were moving away. I panicked.

My circles increased in speed, agitating the water until I accidentally slopped some over the side of the bowl and nearly rode my own wave out onto the parlor's expensive Persian carpet.

Startled, I stilled myself and stared down at the mess, hoping the water wouldn't stain the carpet.

I wasn't worried Johnathon would be upset with me, but he was very proud of the fancy carpet and had worked hard to get it all the way out here. I still couldn't quite fathom the idea it had come from across a salty lake bigger than the sky, but I had no reason to think Johnathon would fib to me. He was a very good and honest human. After all, he had changed my water nearly every day for fifteen years now.

Still, the careless splash bothered me. Fighting off nerves, I swam up and gulped air straight from above the surface to clear my head.

The odd vibration now shook my bowl enough that ripples formed and crashed around the edges. It reminded me of a buffalo herd thundering past our wagon when Johnathon and I traveled out from the East, and I wondered if that was what could be causing the vibration.

That would explain the upset humans, I thought, as I eyed the darker coloration on the carpet where my splashed water had landed.

Clattering sounds caught my attention. Vases, boxes, and curios on the shelves rattled and shook. The tintype photograph of a young Johnathon and his father standing next to a fossil dig fell from the wall. The fossil from the photograph, giant round jaws so large they reached over halfway to the floor, bounced against the wall, looking like they were trying to snap at me.

I hated looking at those giant, ragged teeth. They already gave me nightmares, and seeing them move like this was positively unnerving.

Suddenly my bowl lurched forward, sloshing out more water and sending me swimming desperately downward, trying to stay inside. My little pocket of water in this world of air slid to the edge of the table and threatened to follow the spill down to the floor. My bowl teetered on the edge, forcing me swim away from the edge as hard as I could.

I didn't really think I could stop the fall, but I tried anyway.

My bowl *thunked* back into place and stabilized, water sloshing back and forth violently, bobbing me up and down against my will. As the turbulence slowed, I bellowed my gills, looking down at the now much larger dark spot on the rug. Imagining myself lying there, I was torn between swimming up for another gulp of straight air or trying to bury myself in the rocks at the bottom and hiding.

Movement pulled my attention away from morbid thoughts. Someone tried to open the front door. No—something was coming under the door!

Muddy water foamed through threshold and every crack in the building lower than half the height of a human began spouting silty water. The muck, oozing in, rapidly spread out and engulfed Johnathon's beautiful carpet. In seconds, our little shop was flooded.

"Gasper!"

Johnathon! His voice carried in from the outside. I swam to the top and used my mouth to make popping noises at the surface of the water to let him know I was all right.

"I'm coming, Gasper!" The door flew open and Johnathon splashed in. I was so happy to see him I slapped my tail on the water.

My bowl shuddered again. Johnathon froze. The walls of the house around us groaned and shuddered. The giant fossilized toothy maw shook free from its hanger and fell, splashing down into the brown water.

"Look out!" someone outside shouted.

Sunlight appeared, bright and blindingly shining down through a hole opening up in the roof. Johnathon lunged in my direction but disappeared in a hail of falling debris as the ceiling came crashing down, throwing my bowl, and me along with it, into the darkness of the churning, muddy water.

After what seemed like forever, the rushing water in and around my bowl finally began to slow. I ardently kept myself pressed to the bottom, trying not to get swept out into dangerous waters and crushed by swirling flotsam, but the dirty water was hard to breathe, and I was losing strength.

I couldn't see anything and doubted Johnathon would ever find me in this darkness.

When things were calm as they were likely to get, or at least as calm as they would get before I drowned in the muck, I began cautiously feeling along the inside of the bowl with my nose. In the murky water, the glass was invisible, and I discovered the opening was no longer at the top. I panicked, thinking I was trapped in the bowl forever, and swam in desperate circles. When I tired out and regained my composure, I relaxed and just let the swirling current pull me out.

I sensed the change in the water around me signaling I was no longer within the protection of my bowl, and I pushed my way upward, toward brighter water and sunlight. I surfaced and held my mouth high, sucking in air. It helped, but it was only a temporary solution. I could only breathe this way for a little while before I would be in trouble again. I needed to find clean water and soon.

Pumping my tail, I bobbed up, turning in a circle so I could look around. I'd never seen so much water in all my life. It went as far as I could see in every direction. I wasn't even sure where I was. The town looked different from this angle. I was used to going through it with Johnathon carrying me, which placed me considerably higher in elevation than I currently was. Not to mention the collapsed buildings and water all around changed the look of the town.

An ill feeling came over me. I was looking at the ruins of Johnathon's home. Of course, it was my home as well, but I wasn't nearly attached to it as I knew Johnathon was. I thought of my bowl, lost somewhere in the murk and debris below, and discovered I was wrong. The idea of no more Sunday Luncheons with children smiling, waving, and feeding me bread crumbs left me empty inside.

Then my heart stuttered. Johnathon was under the collapsed house.

A giant splash caught me off guard and I thought I saw those giant teeth from the wall coming at me. I swam for my life, zigzagging away from imaginary snapping jaws trying to pull me in. I couldn't see in the murk, but I raced on in a blind panic anyway, fighting my way through strange currents and eddies caused by water being in places it shouldn't.

I was yards away before I came to my senses. The splash had probably just been more of the house collapsing into the water. This muddy stuff I was swimming in couldn't possibly have any predators in it.

Could it?

The thought startled me. I hadn't needed to avoid predatory fish or birds in years. That had been a nice bonus of choosing to live with Johnathon.

I choked on silt building up in my mouth and pushed up for another gulp of straight air. As I gasped, trying to force the thin air over my gills, I tried to regain my bearings. Dark, swirling water currents pushed against me, and I fought to hold my place. I wasn't sure where I was or where to go. I needed to go back and help Johnathon.

Pushing against the current, I tried to ignore the fact I needed water—clean water—soon.

But I lived in a desert.

One currently flooded with dirty water. The irony did not escape me. One day, Johnathon and I would look back on this and laugh. If Johnathon was all right.

I ignored the thought. Johnathon and I had been through a lot together. He was resourceful and agile. He would be all right. I was sure of it.

I dove and then swam upward fast. Flipping myself completely up and out of the water, I shook off in the air, trying to clear grit from my gills. As I splashed back down I spotted two humans hurriedly wading through knee-deep water toward Johnathon's house. Gratitude flowed through me. They would help him.

"Had to be that dam they were building up north," one of them said.

"Buncha durn fools," the other agreed.

I swam back toward them. I didn't know what I could do to help, but water was my element, not Johnathon's, and if he needed help, I would do whatever I could.

Popping my head up into the air every few feet to keep on course, I was excited to see the men pulling Johnathon up from beneath broken planks of wood. I recognized the men. Roy, the older one, was a bit of a sourpuss, but he was all right. The younger one was Billy. I remembered the time he'd grabbed me by the tail and threatened to eat me to scare the girls.

I didn't like Billy much. And he had bad breath.

"I'm all right, just bruised," I heard Johnathon tell them. "I couldn't get to Gasper in time, though!"

"Just a fish. Not worth dyin' over," Roy said.

Just a fish! Ha! I'll show them! I swam as hard as I could, but Johnathon defended my honor before I could get there.

"Roy, you know better'n that! Gasper's special. She's smart. She started followin' me around like a puppy dog when I was a boy!"

"You mean you carried her 'round like a babe carries a ragdoll."

I was almost to them when something in the debris settled violently, sending waves out and nearly knocking the men over.

"We gotta get away from this," I heard Billy say as I ducked the waves. "Somebody's gonna get killed."

"I can't leave Gasper!"

My heart swelled at the words. Johnathon and I have always been close, but ever since an unusual dog named Scamp, and her equally unusual human, De, had shown Johnathon how to communicate with me, Johnathon and I have been best friends.

As I reached the humans, I launched myself up into the air, slapping my tail rapidly against the water as I went.

"Gasper!" Johnathon cried out.

"Well I'll be a sonofa—"

"We gotta find Gasper's bowl!" Johnathon interrupted Roy. "She can't live in this kind of water!"

I snapped my mouth at him, making popping sounds in agreement, but I hadn't the faintest idea where my bowl was.

"Even if you had a bowl, we ain't got no clean water," Billy said.

I don't like Billy much.

"Find me a bucket, or a jar—anything!" Johnathon began splashing back into the wreckage, pulling up boards and feeling around.

"I don't think that's safe," Billy warned.

A scream startled us all.

"Emma?" Roy turned to look. "Emma!"

Screams of terror joined with the first, both men and women's voices. I couldn't see anyone from where I was, but apparently Roy and Billy could. With worried looks on their faces, they began trying to run through the water toward the sound of the screaming.

"What the...?" Johnathon looked just as concerned, but didn't follow.

I jumped high as I could, trying to see what was going on. At the apex, I managed to spot a group of humans large enough to have been most of the residents of town. They were gathered near the church, which was also surrounded by water. I couldn't stay in the air long enough to understand what they were upset about, only to see they were yelling and pointing.

Then I heard a yowl of terror that was most definitely not human. I turned and saw Charley, the miner's cat who lived in the General Store, sopping wet and clinging to a splintered post broken off from the store's collapsing awning. Her matted fur was so muddy I couldn't even make out the rings on her usually bushy tail. Although we weren't friends, my heart went out to her. Neither a creature of the day nor of the water, the flood had torn her from slumber and thrown her into both.

She cried out again, a terrible sound that told me she was scared beyond reason. She was looking to the same place the humans had been pointing.

Johnathon's voice had a tone I'd never heard before as he continued to stare toward the church. "What is that?"

Perplexed at what could distract everyone from the disaster of a flood and collapsing buildings, I jumped again, trying to see what they could see. As far as I could tell, there was nothing but swirling water where prairie had once been, but I spotted something else before I dropped back down.

Fresh water.

Slapping my tail against the water, I caught Johnathon's attention. When he looked at me, I popped my lips to tell him this was important, and then I took off at top speed for the horse trough I'd spotted. I thought I heard Johnathon splashing after me, but I needed the clean water badly enough I didn't turn around to make sure. I knew he was safe, and that was good enough. I had to take care of myself now.

On days when Johnathon carried me through the town, the General Store hadn't seemed very far away from our home, but swimming the distance against swirling, muddy floodwater felt like the longest journey of my life. I was weakening as I approached the trough. The lack of good water was catching up with me. My tail was weak and my fins felt as though the floating sand and silt had shredded them.

My nose bumped the wooden side of the horse trough and startled me. I'd gone into a daze, forcing myself to continue swimming, and hadn't surfaced to take my bearings. I was lucky to have stayed on course instead of drifting off aimlessly into the murk and fading away from lack of breathable water.

The floodwater was only a couple of inches below the lip of the trough, a sizable jump to be sure, but one I could make. I jumped, already anticipating the feel of clean, fresh, breathable water flowing around my body.

I landed on the edge of the wood, hard. I knocked the bubble out of my swim bladder and gasped in pain as I fell back down into the silty floodwater.

I sank a good ways before I could pull myself together again. Without the air in my swim bladder I wasn't nearly as buoyant, and it was difficult to swim back up. I was fading. With a push of effort, I shot up out of the water as hard as I could—and found myself nowhere near the trough. I had lost my bearings again.

I quickly gulped some air to refill my swim bladder before I splashed back down, but exhaustion began to overtake me. Forcing myself on, I swam back to where I knew the fresh water was, only inches out of my reach, and tried one last time. I didn't even have the strength to get my body all the way out of the water before I began sinking again.

The taste of the floodwater was strong. Curious I hadn't noticed before. So many flavors I didn't recognize. Some tasted like plants. Others like humans. I recognized one—pickles from the giant barrel in the General Store. The children loved the pickles. I didn't much care for the salt, but the acidic vinegar was what made them too much for me. I imagined some of the other flavors were from the herd of Buffalo that had stampeded by, shaking the house down.

Wait…that hadn't been buffalo…

What was I doing…?

Then Johnathon was there, cupping me in his hands and lifting me up out of the darkness.

"I gotcha, Gasper," he said as he lowered me into the gloriously clean water of the horse trough.

I tried to pop my mouth at him, but I was too tired. I tried to pump clean water over my gills, but even that was too much effort. The fresh water was good, but I faded into the darkness anyway.

The strange rumble vibrating through the water in my bowl was giving me dreams of when I'd been living in open water.

Mud! I can't breathe!

I woke thrashing my tail in terror, gills desperately pounding water through me. I could breathe, but I was blind. I couldn't see out of my bowl at all. It took me another moment to realize I was inside of the trough and looking at the featureless, dull-gray tin lining holding the water inside the wooden structure.

My panic faded as I remembered.

Johnathon had saved me.

Excited, I swam up to the surface and popped my lips to call to him if he was close enough hear. The high sides of the trough made it so I could see little more than the top of the General Store and the blue sky above me. When Johnathon didn't respond, I swam to one end of the trough and, careful not to go anywhere near the sides where I might fall out, I leapt up to get a view of what was going on around me.

I heard agitated voices and someone crying, but I found myself looking away from them. Landing, I turned and jumped the other way.

The humans were still gathered at the church, huddled up on the porch, surrounded by floodwater. If the water had retreated any, I couldn't tell. As I fell back down, I began to feel frustrated. I hadn't spotted Johnathon.

"He's gone," a raspy voice snapped from somewhere above me. "He left you. I knew he would."

I swam to the other side of the trough so I could see up to where Charley still clung to the top of the broken post. Half of the General Store was sagging in on itself but leaning away from her, so she didn't seem to be in any danger, but she didn't look good. Her fur was bristly, sticking out in odd ways as muddy water dried and caked on her.

"Humans can't be trusted when you really need them," she cursed. "Always worried about themselves first!" She adjusted her grip on the post, scooting a little higher up and then rubbing the sides of her snout on the wood to scrape drying mud from her whiskers.

"Johnathon is different!" I didn't think she would hear my protest. I didn't have much of a voice, and what little I did have wasn't made for carrying sound through the air, but she heard it.

**68**

"Sure, sure. Just like you're different from all the other fish because you're golden bright and shiny and live in a bubble. Think you're so special?" she barked at me. "He won't be back."

I stopped, stung. I had thought I was special, but I couldn't let her know that. What if she was right? What if Johnathon had left me? Anger and fear surged through me. "I'm just as special as a ring-tailed miner's cat!" I snapped back.

"I'm *not* a cat!"

I already regretted getting angry but couldn't seem to keep my words to myself. "I know that. Everyone knows that. But no one knows just exactly *what* you are! All you do is sneak around at night and scare everyone!"

Charley looked away and didn't respond. Grit in my gills scratched at my attention, so I puffed water over them, opening and closing them as hard as I could a couple of times, trying to get it out. Twisting, I checked each of my fins to see if they were torn. I was surprised to find they were fine. They felt scratched up, though.

I jumped again, trying to get an idea of what was going on with the humans. Just as I cleared the rim of the trough, I spotted something that made me forget to look for anything else. Four loose sheets of paper, covered with smeared colors and symbols, floated, ruined, on top of the brown water. The water had stained the pages and made the ink run, turning all of the beautifully drawn images into unrecognizable blotches.

Landing back in the water, I drifted, stunned. Those were the papers Scamp, De, Johnathon, and I had spent hours working on so that Johnathon and I could communicate. Even if Johnathon came back for me, we might never be able to talk to one another again.

"I'm a ringtail. I'm not a cat," Charley said quietly, startling me out of my despondency. "And I don't sneak around trying to scare everyone. I'm hunting for food."

I turned to look at her. She was looking at me with her big eyes. "I'm sorry I scared you that night. I wasn't going to eat you, I was just curious. I'd never seen a golden fish before."

"Goldfish," I corrected her. "I'm not made out of gold." I fluttered my fins self-consciously. Her words about thinking I was special still stung. Being gold colored was the reason everyone came to visit me in Johnathon's store. But the fear she was right, that Johnathon wouldn't be back, had bitten even deeper. "I didn't know you were looking for food, I'm sorry. I thought they fed you at the General Store."

"Abe used to." She looked away again and her voice grew quiet. "Before he up and left me behind."

I accidently swallowed an air bubble I was mouthing and choked. "Charley." When she didn't look at me, I repeated her name. "Charley, Abe is dead. He passed at the end of last summer."

I saw her stiffen.

"They found him out by the stream. Johnathon said he went peacefully while fishing." I didn't like to think about that part, but humans seemed to think it was a good thing.

Charley's big eyes turned upward, blinking at the bright sun above us. After a long moment her body shuddered with a deep sigh. "Just as well," she said. "He wouldn't have liked being eaten by a shark anyway."

It took a moment for her words to register.

"A shark?"

Charley nodded her head. "Yup. That's what everyone is screaming about over there. There's a shark circling the church."

"You must be mistaken. Sharks can't…" I was at a loss for words.

"Your human always says those bones up on the wall in your store, that big mouth full of teeth, came from a shark."

"Well yeah, but—"

"Well that thing swimming around out there has a whole mouth full of those teeth." She pointed in the direction of the church with her snout. "So I'd say it's a shark."

Charley stiffened, her gaze locking on something in the direction of the humans. Clumps of her fur swelled in lumps as it tried to bristle while stuck together by mud. "It's coming back!" she shrieked, scuttling up to the topmost edge of her perch.

I watched in horror, unable to see anything but Charley as she cowed. Growling low in her throat, she let loose a small but vicious roar that reminded me of a puma I'd once heard, then a giant shape appeared over the edge of the trough, leaping through the air for her. Horrible teeth snapped just below her tail as the great gray fish arced through the air and splashed back down, sending droplets of filthy water raining down into my fresh water haven.

I was knocked sideways as waves slammed into the trough. The monster leaped at Charley a second time. In spite of being off kilter, I got a better look at the beast. No doubt about it, it was a shark. One big enough eat a large human in only a bite or two.

As more muddy water splashed down upon me, I gaped in shock. I could see right through the creature. It was a ghost. It had to be. How else could a giant water-bound predator be out here in the desert?

Scamp, the unusual dog who had helped Johnathon learn to communicate with me, had said her mother hunted ghosts, when she wasn't herding sheep. I can't honestly say I'd believed the stories Scamp told, but I hadn't disregarded them either. I accepted them as something Scamp thought was real, and that was good enough for me.

I thought of those teeth coming at me in the ruins of Johnathon's house. Could it possibly be?

Charley roared again, snapping me out of my shock as the shark jumped for her a third time. The fur on Charley's tail fluttered under the shark's nose before the monster fell back to the water. The waves shook the damaged awning and rang the dangling alarm bell.

My scales constricted in fear. My nightmare had come true.

The fur on Charley's back slowly laid down and her growl quieted. Watching the direction of her gaze, I guessed the shark had given up and swam back toward the humans. A chorus of screams confirmed my thought.

A stream of expletives, the likes I had never heard and most of which I didn't understand, erupted from Charley as she shook herself off and readjusted her grip on the post. "See if I don't!" she finished and spat in the direction of the shark.

Gunshots echoed across the water, and I had to jump to see what was going on.

The church, damaged just as badly as all the other buildings, listed to one side. The humans struggled to fit on the small porch without putting themselves in danger by going into the building. The ghost shark thrashed in the water, trying to get at them. Two men were shooting while a third swung a rake at its gnashing jaws, trying to keep it away from a group of screaming children huddled at the edge of the porch.

I fell back to my little pond of safety just as I recognized that the man with the rake was Johnathon.

Now I knew why he hadn't come back. He was protecting the children. I would have done the same.

Jumping for another look, I saw the ghost shark bite at the rake and nearly pull Johnathon into the water. He wasn't going to be able to hold it off for long.

I had to do something to help Johnathon. I puffed my scales in agitation as I dodged streamers of mud floating down through my clean water, courtesy of the shark's splashing. I turned too quickly and ran into one of the murky streaks, which irritated me even more. I snorted to clear away the taste of pickles it had brought in with it. I hated that salty—

Suddenly, I got an idea.

Leaping up, I looked toward the damaged General Store and spotted what I searched for: the pickle barrel.

Knocked askew and out of its normal place just outside the door, it now stood mostly upright, wedged between the outside wall and one of the twisted poles still holding up the awning. Titled toward me, I could see it was still full of brine with pickles five times my size floating in it.

"Charley!" I called to get the miner's cat's attention—Excuse me. I mean, the ringtail's attention. "Charley!"

She turned those big soulful eyes down to me. The wet fur around them told me she'd been crying.

"I know how to save the humans!" I said. "But I need your help!"

The barking erased any last vestiges of doubt in my mind that Charley wasn't a cat. From her vantage, her voice carried clearly across the water to the church where the humans huddled together. And where the shark still circled.

"I'll give you such a what-for, you ugly tube of teeth! Come on back here and see!" Charley barked at the shark. "You sure this will work? Salt really banishes ghosts?" she quickly asked down at me.

"If what Scamp told me was true, this should work!"

Charley barked some more and then turned to me again. "What if I forget the words?"

"Don't worry. You won't."

"What if it's not enough salt?"

"Pickles are the saltiest thing I know!"

"Oh, my. It's coming back!" Charley's barks turned shrill as she edged high as she could go up the pole. "Go, Gasper," she yelled. "Go, go, go!"

I flushed one last wave of clean water across my gills and raced for the side of the trough, building up as much speed as I could, then I leaped high into the air. Up, and out, over the lip of the trough.

In my peripheral vision, I could see the shark behind me. It was so much closer than I'd expected, but it was too late to change my mind now.

As I fell to the muddy water outside the trough, I popped my lips and swished my tail to get its attention. The shark didn't notice and continued for Charley. Maybe I was too small.

Charley shrieked in terror, nearly falling off the post.

"Over here you big galoot!" I jumped again, slapping my tail as hard as I could and splashing water at the shark. That got his attention, and I got my first good look at his teeth. They were each bigger than I was. Much bigger.

And I swear they were the same ones from the wall—my nightmare lived.

I panicked and swam hard as I could. I had to get away from that monster. The muddy murk of the floodwater was worse than I remembered. I couldn't see anything. I was afraid of running into debris, but I was afraid of those teeth even more.

When I couldn't breathe the silty water anymore, I risked a trip upward for a gulp of air.

"The other way!" I heard Charley squealing as I broke the surface. "You went the wrong way!"

The shark broke the water not ten feet away as I realized I'd forgotten to follow my own plan. Hard black eyes gleamed at me, and I dove back into the water wondering if all ghosts had soulless eyes. The water behind me felt cold as I adjusted my course for the pickle barrel.

There was no way I could escape this monster, but if I could just reach the barrel before it ate me, maybe I could save Johnathon. That would be good enough.

I flipped up into the air, gasping for breath as I soared. The shark erupted up behind me, moving faster than I ever could have. Only its extreme power saved me. It leaped too hard and overshot where I was already falling back to the water.

It fell back in ahead of me, its tail slicing through the water and creating eddies that sent me spinning away, disoriented and lost. Sharp grit, cut from the desert winds instead of smoothing water, filled my gills and cut at my fins and eyes. I fought the current created by the passing of the beast, trying to force myself back up to the surface to get my bearings.

I heard Charley scream before I could see what was going on. When I finally got my head out of the water, the post Charley had been sitting on was bare.

Charley was gone, and it was my fault. She had trusted me, she trusted my plan, and I…I had panicked and tried to save myself.

Swirling water caught my attention and I spotted the shark's dorsal fin heading back toward the church. Back toward Johnathon.

"No!" I shouted. "No!" That monster could not have my Johnathon. "Over here!" It continued to swim away. "Over here!" I splashed and jumped trying to get its attention.

I shouted until I couldn't see it anymore, even knowing my meager fish voice couldn't carry that far, especially in the thinness of air.

More screams came from the humans.

I choked on the gritty water. I didn't know what to do.

The smell of pickles filled my nose. I'd almost managed to get to the barrel. It just hadn't been close enough.

My strength was fading as I turned to look at the barrel, only a few feet from me now. The awning had collapsed further and, tauntingly, the barrel was tipped even farther over. I could easily jump into it myself now.

I felt like doing just that as I heard the humans scream and wondered if one of them was Johnathon. That made me wonder if Charley had suffered.

Then I noticed the alarm bell. Hanging from the falling awning, it was nearly all the way down to the water now. And the bell was a lot louder than my voice.

Maybe I could still save someone. If there was a way I could help, I had to try. All I had to do was get the ghost shark in the salty pickle juice and say the words Scamp had taught me, right?

I swam for the bell at full speed, leaped, and slapped my tail against the iron lip.

The sound was pathetic. I almost couldn't hear the bell over the wet sound of my tail slap. I tried again with no better result.

Frustrated, I slapped the water with my tail.

"Gasper? Is that you?" A timid voice came from somewhere over my head. I swam out from under the awning to see who was above me.

"Charley! You're all right!"

"It almost got me!" Charley hung her nose over the edge of the tilted roof and looked down at me, her eyes big and scared. "I made the biggest jump of my life to get here! And look!" She turned and showed me the bare pink tip of her tail where ringed fur was missing.

"I've got to save the humans," I said, "but I can't ring the bell. Can you do it?"

Her eyes widened, something I didn't think was possible, and she backed away. "No! No, no, no!"

"Just ring the bell, and then get back up there where the shark can't see you. I'll do the rest. I promise I won't mess up this time."

An extra loud scream from the humans punctuated my plea.

"Please Charley. I can't do it alone."

"Just one ring?"

"Just one!" I agreed.

Charley leaned over the edge and examined the bell, looking for a way to come down. I choked on some grit and spit it out, trying to ignore my fading energy from lack of clean water.

"Okay," Charley agreed, and then she climbed down onto the bell. With front paws hooked on the awning, she pushed the bell with her back legs, slowly rocking it back and forth.

"Good job," I told her. "You can do this."

Pushing and gaining momentum, she continued until the clapper finally struck and rung. And then she pushed again, ringing the bell again, and again.

"You did it!" I cried.

"This time we're gonna get that—"

The bell clap covered her words, but I was sure I knew what she meant.

Charley climbed back up on the roof of the awning and stood on her hind legs, looking out toward the church. "Be ready, Gasper! It's coming fast this time!"

"Tell me when to go," I said.

"Ready…"

I took a gulp of pure air and puffed my scales.

"… set …"

I was ready. The ghost shark didn't have a chance this time.

"… go! Go, Gasper, go!"

Trusting Charley, I leaped from the water next to the bell, slapping my tail and making all the noise I could to get the ghost's attention. I saw it surface just as I fell back down. When I felt the pressure of the water it pushed ahead of itself, I leaped again, as far as I could go.

The ghost shark leaped after me and I could feel its coldness catching up with me. The barrel was only a little more than one more leap away. I could do this. Teeth gnashed in the water behind me. I skimmed up to the surface to see where the barrel was. My timing had to be perfect for a jump like this.

I flipped my tail as hard as I could, lifting myself up into the air just as I felt the void of the shark's dagger-riddled jaws upon me. At the last possible instant, I drug my tail, the friction against the water dropping me right back down and bringing me to a dead stop.

The shark, anticipating my jump, followed the arc I would have made and landed headfirst, jamming its oversized snout into the pickle barrel.

I started trying to chant the words Scamp had taught me, but I was too out of breath. They came out broken and stuttered.

The shark thrashed and pickles and brine sloshed out through its ghostly body.

Somehow my words got stronger, louder than I'd ever been able to speak. They weren't just my words. They were Charley's, too. As we spoke in unison, the ghost fought to free itself from the barrel, rolling and splashing all around.

And then an even stronger voice joined in.

Johnathon appeared next to me, chanting the same words. He must have learned them from De.

The ghost shark managed one last mighty flip of its tail, spinning the whole barrel around before the power of the words overtook it. There was a bright flash, and I thought I saw something swimming up toward the sky, and then the ghost was gone.

Johnathon held a cigar tin down low to the water and motioned for me to jump in. I wasn't crazy about cigars, but I trusted Johnathon, so I jumped.

The relief was instant and blissful. Later Johnathon told me it was holy water.

The fire crackled in our new pot-bellied stove. I dozed as I watched it from my new crystal bowl. The sun was setting and the coming night was chill. Our new store had been finished last week, just in time for the fall weather.

Charley's nose peeked out of the box Johnathon had made for her and placed by the stove so it would stay warm. She waggled her whiskers at me and headed straight to the bowl of food Johnathon put out for her. After a quick sniff and a smile of approval, she stood on her back legs and pointed at the framed newspaper hanging on the wall. With a quick wink and a smile, she headed out to search for prey, just to keep up her skills. At least that's what she said when she went out last night.

I looked back to the newspaper on the wall. It had an image of me, Charley, and Johnathon all together under the headline *Town Heroes*. I liked looking at it. It made me happy.

A knock on the door woke me just as I was about to fall asleep. It was a little late for visitors.

"Coming!" Johnathon came out from the back room and answered the door. "Billy! Come on in." Johnathon held the door open.

"Look what I found." Billy stepped in, holding up the fossilized jaws that had once hung on our store wall.

I don't like Billy much.

At least if those jaws come alive again, I know I'm the fish for the job, and I'll have Charley here to help me.

Originally published in Ghost Hunting Critters by Inkwolf Press, September 1, 2017

Characters and concepts from Ghost Hunting Dog/Eye of the Dog world of J.A. Campbell used with permission.

# SMOTE BY RED LIGHTNING

Annabelle Buescher was fourteen and laden heavily with first child when her husband was smote by God. She was sure it was God's retribution for more than just one reason, not the least of which was that it happened only moments after Annabelle cursed Joseph for spending her dowry on the whores in town. Her husband, being a good, God-fearing man of nearly three times her age and experience, knew the place of a woman in his household and had immediately beaten Annabelle for her sass and then set off to find a switch the thickness of his thumb for a proper punishment.

Trembling with fear, blood running from her nose and split lip, her swollen belly cramping from the repeated punches, Annabelle had crawled to the doorway to watch Joseph Buescher march through the tall grass, straight down to the river willows. He made a great show of looking for a proper switch, cut one, and then raised it into the air for her to see.

"That was when God smote him," Annabelle said, chin held high as she recounted her story to Marshal Brawner. The gleam in her blackened eye was one of righteous satisfaction. "The lightning bolt took him in the top of the head."

Brawner, looking at the welts on Annabelle's face, had no doubts as to why she was not upset over her husband's death.

"But the lightning bolt was *red!*" Father Crane excitedly nodded. The grin on his face was out of place for the normally stern-looking old man, even had they not been talking about the death of one of his flock. He'd heard the story first and brought Annabelle straight over to tell Marshal Brawner. Not, Brawner suspected, because there had been a death so much as because Father Crane wanted to report an Act of God right here in their little part of the world.

"Is that right?" Marshal Brawner asked. The wooden sidewalk creaked under his weight as he adjusted to put the sun at his back in order to get a better look at Annabelle's bruised face.

"Not only was it red," Annabelle answered, "it came in straight as an arrow. Not at all like regular lightning. This was *Holy Lightning.*" She kept one arm cupped around her enlarged abdomen as she spoke. The other arm lifted to point a finger angrily at the sky. "Sent directly from heaven to punish Joseph for his sins!"

Brawner turned to watch a wagon roll by, concentrating on the horses pulling it. Still little more than a child, Annabelle didn't yet have the bearing to pull off being a high-handed woman of God, and her act of indignation, regardless of the signs of violence on her face, was near ludicrous. She deserved better than to be laughed at even if she did look like a child with a pillow under her dress.

"You are looking a little red yourself, ma'am," Brawner told her when he was sure he could keep back the smile. "Perhaps you should sit and rest for a bit. Maybe get that lip attended to."

"Yes." Still holding her belly, Annabelle used her other hand to fan her face. "I am feeling a bit flushed, what with my situation and all. And of course, you know that's why I came to town. I am in no condition to get rid of Joseph's body, and there is no one else at the ranch to help me."

"Get rid of…?" the marshal asked.

"Well, you don't think he deserves a good Christian burial after God Himself has passed judgement like that, do you? But

I can't leave his body there to stink and rot, so I need help getting rid of it."

"You believe her story?" Marshal Brawner asked Father Crane when they were out of earshot. They had taken Annabelle to lie down at Father Crane's house, where the priest's wife was now watching over the pregnant woman.

"You heard her! Red lightning!" Father Crane's eyes were alight with the possibility that God had manifested so near and in such a tangible way. His smile faded as he studied the marshal. "You don't believe her?"

"I tend to believe that people suffer out here," Brawner answered. "Things don't usually seem to go right for most them. If she'd come in and said he was struck by lightning, I would have believed her. Even if she said it was God sent the lightning to smite the man. But to embellish the story with a red lightning bolt that flew straight as an arrow? Well, now I've got to wonder what really happened."

"What do you mean, 'what really happened?'"

"I mean I have to wonder if she killed him herself."

"Killed—? Why would you even think such a thing?"

"You heard her story, Father, and you saw the beating on her face. Why *wouldn't* you think so?"

Father Crane drove a one-horse wagon, following Marshal Brawner and the three other men on horseback. Brawner had asked the men to come help deal with Joseph's corpse. Out of deference to the old priest, the marshal kept the horses at a walk rather than galloping to the Buescher ranch as he would have preferred. At this pace there was little chance they'd be home by dark.

Had there been no mention of God, the old man likely couldn't have been coaxed to come out to the body even were it still alive and in need of last rites, but after Annabelle's talk of 'Holy Lightning', the priest wouldn't be turned away. His arguments for attending had ranged from the need to assess Joseph Buescher's suitability for a Christian funeral to perhaps putting the body on display as a warning to other sinners, and then even something about the body being of interest to the church as a holy relic. He'd also gone back and forth about the sins of adultery and being a disobedient wife. The non-stop clatter of excited babble finally got under Brawner's skin, and he made sure he was in the lead on the way to the ranch, so he didn't have to listen to the improvised sermon anymore.

Once a week in church was bad enough.

"You really think ol' Joe was struck down by God hisself?" Art Smith asked as they rode alongside one another.

"As much as any man ever struck by lightning was," Brawner answered.

Art nodded and went back to looking at the countryside, wide-eyed. Art was still young, not yet twenty, and the news had seemed to instill a sense of wonder, and a bit of fear, in him. He wasn't Brawner's first choice of men to have along, but Art had been standing next to Will Darcy when Brawner asked Will to come, and it was hard to turn down a willing volunteer for what might end up being shovel-work.

Darcy, on the other hand, was a good fellow. Quick to work, work hard, and work long, the blacksmith was also about as honest and forthright a man as Brawner had ever met. Truth be told, Brawner asked him along to get his opinion of the whole situation. He needed less…judgmental advice than he was likely to get from Father Crane.

The third man, the one now getting an earful of religion from Father Crane, was another hard worker and good man. Despite having been called "Jon Jon" and repeatedly referred to as a heathen several times in the last hour, he was still politely listening to the ranting old priest, even going so far as to have dropped back to ride alongside the wagon so the priest would stop shouting to him. The man's real name was Gong Lee—at least, that was a close as Brawner could pronounce it. He was also the closest thing Brawner had to a best friend.

It had become Brawner's Saturday afternoon ritual to have lunch with Gong's family and entertain the children by trying to pronounce their names. Brawner just couldn't hear the difference in what they said from what he said. The only name he could ever get right was Gong's wife's: Chen.

"You think, if God's in the mood to strike more folk down, that he's more likely to pick one of us on account of we're going to where Joe got smited?" Art asked, breaking Brawner's reverie. The man sounded nervous, as if he'd just realized he had a sin to hide.

"Now that's a good question." Brawner raised his voice over the sounds of the horses and the creaking wagon. "Father Crane? Art here's got a question for you!" He looked to Art and said, "Why don't you switch places with Gong and ask the preacher-man that question."

"Switch with who?" Art genuinely looked confused.

"Jon Jon," Brawner said, trying to hide his disgust at using the name. "The laundry man."

"Oh, yeah." Art kneed his horse to the side and dropped back as Gong rode forward, passing Darcy to catch up with Brawner.

"Thanks, Brawner," Gong whispered. "I owe you one."

"Nope. You and Chen been feeding me for going on two years now. You owe me nothing."

"You eat Chen's cooking so I don't have to eat so much. I owe you plenty."

Father Crane, now that he had a new set of ears to preach to, started his entire contemplative sermon over, right back to whether or not Joseph deserved a Christian burial.

"For a holy man, he sure seems awful excited about someone getting killed, doesn't he?" Brawner muttered.

Joseph Buescher's forehead had a hole in it so big and clean that they could all see right through it to the ground underneath. The sink of char could still be made out over the growing smell of the body having lain in the sun all day. It was that smell that made Art turn to the bushes and puke.

"I'll be damned if that's a bullet hole," Darcy said.

The old priest didn't react to the curse. He'd been so excited to get out of the wagon and see the body that Brawner was sure he hadn't even crossed himself at the sight of the dead man, a habit as common to the priest as twisting mustache was to others.

"Looks like he fell straight back when he died," Gong said.

Brawner nodded. "I agree. With both of you."

"He's still holding the switch, just like Annabelle said," Father Crane said, pointing to the man's hand, as if it proved the rest of her story true.

"Her footprints are all over here." Brawner pointed out the woman's smaller tracks. "She could have put it in his hand."

"Maybe." Darcy leaned close to look at the wound in Joseph's head. "But I don't think she did this. I don't know how anyone could do this."

Father Crane didn't say anything. The wonder and awe in his face made him look struck dumb.

"Hey, fellas, look at that!" Art called their attention to a smoldering hole in the trunk of a big cottonwood tree on the other side of the river. "Looks like lightning hit that tree!"

"Thought she said it went arrow straight?" Gong asked. "This would be more like what I would expect from lightning. Hit the man and bounce off, then hit something else. Like an angry snake."

Brawner looked from the hole in the corpse's head to hole in the tree and then back again.

"Darcy," he said, "help me stand the body up."

"Stand it up?"

"You're not going to move him!" Father Crane was appalled.

Brawner eyed the priest. "You think we need to leave him here in the weeds?"

"Well, no… but…" The old man seemed frantic.

Gong looked sideways at the priest. "You're not thinking to build a shrine, are you?"

Father Crane's eyes brightened as though that was exactly the idea he'd been looking for.

"Why," Gong continued, "would you build a shrine to an adulterer God struck dead? Makes no sense to honor the dishonored."

The priest looked like he was going to argue, then his shoulders slumped, and he closed his gaping mouth.

Bending to lift the body from under the arms, Brawner motioned Darcy to help. The two picked the corpse up into a standing position as the priest backed away. "Let's put him in his tracks," Brawner said, indicating to move the body forward about a foot.

Lifting, they carried it a step forward and put its shoes in the very tracks they had left hours earlier. Brawner tried to steady the body with one hand while lifting the head with the other but couldn't.

"Art—?" Brawner looked at the ashen-faced man, sighed and turned to Gong. "Gong, would you hold ol' Joe up please?"

Gong, who was over a foot shorter than Brawner and the corpse, stepped up and did his best to help Darcy steady the body.

Brawner stood in front of the corpse and lifted its head up straight, looking it in the face.

"Whatcha doin'?" Art asked, clearly repelled at the idea of someone having their face inches from the face of a dead body with a two-inch hole through its head.

"Sighting it in," Brawner answered.

"What?"

Ignoring Art, Brawner looked back toward the house, to where Annabelle would have been standing when the lightning hit, and then adjusted the corpse's head to be looking there. Looking through the hole in the head, he found it lined up perfectly with the hole in the tree on the other side of the river.

"Darcy, can you hold his head right there?"

"Like this?" Darcy asked, grabbing a fistful of hair on the top.

"Yup." Brawner walked around the two men to the backside of the corpse, checked the alignment of the holes, and sighted to where he thought the lightning must have come from to come in straight as an arrow from that angle.

Father Crane seemed absolutely dismayed by Brawner's actions, but he didn't voice any complaints.

"Whatcha see?" Darcy asked. "Don't look like it come from Heaven."

"Nope. Looks like it came from the clearing on the top of that hill right there."

Father Crane and Art both turned to look as well, the priest suddenly remembering to cross himself.

"I don't remember ever seeing that clearing before," Darcy said, "and I've hunted this land for five years."

"Me neither," Art added.

"I don't remember it either," Brawner added, "and I helped build the house."

"God Almighty, something just gave me the woollies bad!" Art looked nervously to the other men.

Brawner noticed Father Crane crossing himself again and looking like he was going to do it a third time.

"I have a bad feeling," Gong said, looking as though he wanted to hide behind the corpse he was helping hold up. "Very bad."

"Well," Brawner interrupted the moment before everyone ruined themselves, "I'm pretty sure Miss Annabelle doesn't want him buried on the property, so let's get Joe into the wagon and take him back to town where Father Crane can figure out what to do with him." He bent down and grabbed the body by the boots, lifting it up, and the three of them carried it to the wagon before unceremoniously heaving it in.

They all stood and stared for a moment before Brawner grabbed the edge of an old canvass sheet and pulled it over the corpse.

When it was out of sight, Art seemed to come back to life. "We ready to go?"

Marshal Brawner shook his head. "I reckon I need to go check out that clearing. I'd feel remiss in my duties as lawman if I didn't."

Art looked stricken. "I-I'd forgotten all about it," he said as he turned and looked back towards the hill.

"Me, too." Gong frowned. "My very bad feeling just came back."

"You think someone shot a bolt of red lightning at Joe's head?" Darcy asked. It was the first time Brawner had ever heard the blacksmith sound nervous.

"I don't know what to think." Brawner looked at the men around him. He felt his own irrational anxiety about going up there. "Father Crane? Any advice on this situation?"

The priest crossed himself again. He looked very old and frail. "I've encountered the Lord many times, many ways in my life, but this, this doesn't feel like him. I'm not sure what happened here, but I think Annabelle may have misunderstood it."

Shaking his head, Father Crane said, "I would strongly recommend that you don't go up that hill, Marshal Brawner."

Looking at each man, Brawner noted that only he and Art carried sidearms. The priest, unlike most people, didn't carry a rifle when he took to the wagon. Gong didn't carry weapons. He'd once told Brawner they attracted the attention of people looking to make trouble—and there was always someone looking to make trouble with a Chinaman. Darcy had a hunting rifle at home, but he hadn't expected to be hunting today.

That left Art. Brawner didn't think he'd trust Art not to panic and shoot when he shouldn't.

He decided not to ask any of them to come along.

"Won't take but a minute to check it out," he said. "Why don't you all start heading back? If you leave now, you might make it while it's still light enough to see. I'll catch up."

"I'll come with you," Gong said quickly.

"Me too," said Darcy.

"Art," Brawner said before the man had a chance to chime in, "do me a favor and accompany Father Crane back to town? If you beat us back, he'll need help with Joe."

Art looked relieved and nodded, turning and immediately heading for his horse.

Father Crane shuffled to the wagon and climbed up into the spring seat. He looked uncomfortably at the three men he was leaving behind before crossing himself. "God watch over you." He glanced up the hill at the clearing and then flicked the reins.

Darcy, Gong, and Brawner watched Art follow the wagon down the road until the silence became oppressive.

"Well," Brawner looked back and forth between his two friends, "let's get this over with."

"Goddamn," Darcy muttered, more willing to curse now that Father Crane was gone. "I'd already forgotten what we were gonna do again already. Something mighty ill-boding about that clearing."

"I agree," Gong said.

Brawner looked back and forth between his two friends and weighed the feeling in his gut against the way he imagined they must feel.

"Let's go into the house," he said. "Ol' Joe had to have a firearm of some sort. I can't imagine he'd be objecting to us borrowing it while looking for his killer."

The town was silent and dark as the three men rode in after midnight. Brawner, Darcy, and Gong split up wordlessly and each headed home, their horses following familiar trails by feel more than by the dim starlight.

Brawner arrived home easily and went about the business of stabling his horse without bothering to light a lantern. When he was done, he went into the house and found a pouch of tobacco and a pipe and brought them out to the rocking chair on the porch, as was his wont at the end of long days. The quiet creak of the rocking chair and a light rustle of leaves in the trees were the only sounds as he packed the pipe and struck a match.

The flare of matchlight, bright as the sun before his face, startled him, and he dropped the match into his lap and then near knocked the rocker over backwards as he tried to get away from the flame.

Eyes wild, Brawner panted for air as his heart threatened to explode out of his chest. He searched the night frantically for danger, confused by his own sudden fear. There was nothing but the match burning on the wooden porch planks at his feet.

Brawner crushed the match with his boot and the world was dark again, but he was finally awake.

The sun couldn't come early enough for Brawner, so he left home before it was up, arriving at the center of town just as the dawn grew light enough to make out the lettering of the General Store's sign.

He stopped his horse in the middle of road and looked around, not sure what to do.

Brawner *needed* to do something, but he had no pressing business, especially this time of day. He thought about going over to see Gong, but he didn't want to wake the whole family for…what?

For some idiocy he couldn't quite put his finger on, that's what. Why did he feel the need to talk to Gong so badly?

A banging door caught his attention, and he turned just in time to see someone stumble out of the bath house. No, stumble wasn't right. They were tossed.

The man tripped down the steps but managed to keep his feet. A hat, coat, and a boot flew through the air at him.

"You can have the other boot when you come back to pay!" an angry woman called after him before slamming the door.

Brawner barely caught a glimpse of her in the lamplight before she was gone. It had been Macy Newhart, better known as Goldie, the madame who ran the bath house/brothel. Apparently, she had seen Brawner as well, as the door opened back up a crack, and then widened as she looked out.

"Marshal Brawner?" she called, squinting into the dim morning light.

The man picking up his hat and coat suddenly looked up, startled.

"Ma'am." Brawner tipped the brim of his hat to her.

Goldie opened the door wide. The light inside backlit her, showing her figure through the flimsy gown she wore and making her yellow hair glow the way Brawner imagined an angel's would. She pulled her gown tight around herself and stepped out onto the porch. "May I speak with you a moment please?"

The man in the road grabbed at his boot and raced toward the stable.

Brawner stifled a chuckle as Goldie dismissively waved a hand at the man. "It ain't about him," she said. "Let him go. He'll be back. His wedding ring is in that other boot."

Brawner dismounted and led his horse to the hitching post before tying the reins up.

"You want to talk out here?" he asked.

"No. It's too chilly out. Come inside. I'll make you some coffee."

"That would be kind of you." Brawner followed her into the bath house and shut the door behind him as she poured coffee from an already heated pot set on top of the wood stove used to heat the water for the baths.

"You were out at Joseph Buescher's farm last night?"

Brawner started at the thought. He *had* been at the farm. He *knew* he had been at the farm. That's what he had wanted to talk to Gong about, but…for some reason the thought was slippery and hard to hold on to. He nodded as he again tried to remember leaving the farm. He couldn't remember leaving, and that's what was bothering him.

"Tell me what happened to Joseph." Goldie's slate blue eyes were cold and hard as stone as she handed him the steaming cup of coffee.

"Well…" He thought of the perfect hole in the man's head. "I can't rightly say I know what happened to him."

"I do. She killed him," Goldie said with vehemence. "That lying little whore killed him!"

"Whoa. Hold on, now."

"No, you listen to me. Here's what you don't know—what she won't tell you. Joseph never laid with her. *Never.* She wouldn't let him, claimed the sickness every time he tried."

Brawner sat the coffee on the table without taking a drink. "Never?"

"Never. That child ain't his. Her pa was some high muckamuck who paid Joseph to take her to a convent to get the disgrace away from the family when she wouldn't tell who the father was. Of course, she didn't want to go. Instead, she cajoled Joseph into marrying her, telling him to keep the money what was supposed to go to the convent, coaxing him with her feminine charms, promising to be the best wife anyone ever had, promising she had learned her lesson and saying that she had fallen in love with him."

Goldie took a breath and seemed to realize she was being a poor hostess. She gestured for Brawner to sit and then seated herself at the table across from him. "She held out until they were married, saying reason was they weren't married, of course, and then, when they were married, she still refused, saying she was sick with the child she already had."

"How do you know all of this?" Brawner asked, finally taking a sip of the strong coffee. The morning light was beginning to come in the windows and the room had taken on a dusky light that made it harder to see than it had been with just the lamplight.

"Joseph told me. When he came to…to relieve the pressure of having a wife that ain't a wife who's with child that ain't his." She stared at Brawner for a moment, watching to see how much he understood. "He was a good man."

"He beat her," Brawner said matter-of-factly.

"And you wouldn't?" Goldie asked. "She was a whore he rescued from a choice between a life of sin and scorn or a life of solitude in a church prison, and this is how she repays him?" Tears formed in Goldie's eyes, gilded with the light from the lamp's flame. "She's probably already making plans to head back east with Joseph's money and meet up with her bastard's father."

Goldie suddenly slammed her hand on the table, the sound filling the room like a gunshot. "She killed him! God damn it! I know she did. She killed him…and—and I loved him." She broke into a sob and looked away.

Brawner sat silently watching her trembling shoulders as he considered her words.

"Goldie?" A timid woman's voice called from upstairs.

"Go back to bed, Lilly," Goldie said, clearing her voice and trying to sound strong. "It's okay."

The sun was up by the time Brawner got to Father Crane's. The priest's wife was already hanging wash out to dry in the morning breeze, and she stopped to greet him. "God bless you on this wonderful morning, Marshal."

"And you, Mrs. Crane." Brawner dismounted and tied his horse up in front of the house. "Is Mrs. Buescher around?"

"Annabelle was up for breakfast but may have lain back down. Let me go check for you."

"Thank you, Ma'am." Brawner stayed next to his horse as the woman hurried up the steps and into the house. After only a moment, she poked her head out and waved him in.

The house was cozy and better furnished than most, with ample space to host important guests, traveling clergy, or other needful members of the flock. Annabelle was seated at the table and smiled pleasantly at Brawner as he entered. The bruising had spread to both of her eyes and the swelling on the bridge of her nose looked painful.

"Good morning, Marshal." She spoke carefully with a swollen lip that looked ready to split again.

"Mrs. Buescher. I was wondering if you and I could have some words."

"Of course."

Brawner turned to look at Mrs. Crane, who was still standing at the edge of the room. "Thank you, Ma'am."

The older woman looked flustered, not wanting to be dismissed from her own home, to leave an unmarried man and woman alone together, or both.

Brawner looked back to Annabelle. "You might not want this for other ears."

"I'm sure we'll be alright, Mrs. Crane." Annabelle nodded to the woman. The priest's wife hesitated and then left.

Brawner was sure she wouldn't go far.

He moved to the table. "May I sit?"

"Please do."

"I have to ask you a few uncomfortable questions."

"I didn't kill him. You saw the hole in his head. He was struck down by God."

"Is it true the baby you carry isn't his?"

Annabelle reddened. "He told stories to that whore he was spending all our money on, didn't he?"

"Is it true?"

Emotions colored her face and she grimaced, tears of anger forming in her eyes.

"I'll assume that means yes."

"It's not my fault!" The emotions broke through and Annabelle nearly began wailing. "Why did this happen to me? What did I do to deserve this?"

The sound of near hysterical woman immediately brought Mrs. Crane back into the house, just as Annabelle confessed her deepest secret.

"I never had relations with anyone, Marshal! Not with anyone! Pa wouldn't believe me, but it's true! No one believes me!"

Marshal Brawner, blocked at the door by Father Crane, shook his head wearily. "Do you realize how you sound?" He resisted the urge to take a step back from the agitated priest.

"But what if it's true?" Father Crane insisted. "What if—?"

"What if I would have brought this tall tale to you? You wouldn't have entertained it for a moment." Brawner turned to face the priest's wife, standing in the foyer. "You're the one who told him she said that, you talk some sense into him."

Brawner stepped around Father Crane and left the house. He had to admit his feelings were nearly as confused as Father Crane's—but about something else entirely.

Until he had started talking about Joseph Buescher's death again, specifically about the hole in his head, he had forgotten, again, that he'd wanted to talk to Gong and Darcy about leaving the Buescher ranch. Somehow the idea kept slipping away from him, and he didn't like that one bit.

He untied his horse, mounted up, and rode straight to the blacksmith's at full gallop before he could get distracted again.

"Where's the fire?" Darcy called as Brawner reined his horse in, kicking up a cloud of dust.

"I need to talk to you," Brawner said, hopping down and looping the reins on the hitching pole in front of the water trough.

"What about?" The blacksmith sat down the horseshoes he'd been sorting with a concerned look on his face.

"About… God damn it!" Brawner gave into frustration and stomped in the dirt.

"Somethings got you riled!" Darcy laughed. "You finally find a woman?"

Woman… Annabelle… murder…

Thoughts connected through Brawner's mind again.

"About what happened last night!" Brawner near shouted, trying to get it out before he lost it again. "Do you remember leaving the Buescher place last night?"

The grin on Darcy's face vanished and he went pale. "I don't want to talk about that." His voice was deadly.

"Don't want to talk about what?" Brawner stepped closer. "Do you remember? I can't remember shit!"

The big man was shaking now, and he moved back from Brawner.

"What happened to us? Do you remember going up to that clearing? The last thing I remember is going into the house and getting Buescher's rifle."

Darcy turned his head to look at something and his mouth gaped. In the corner, Brawner spotted Buescher's lever action repeating rifle leaning against the wall.

"You don't remember either, do you?" Brawner asked. He didn't wait for an answer. "I have to go see Gong."

Mounting back up, Brawner called to Darcy. "You coming? Or are you content to stay here feeling scared to death about something you don't even know what is?"

The blacksmith took a deep breath and then stood tall. An angry snarl crossed his face, and he marched to Buescher's rifle and snatched it from the corner. "I'm right behind you."

Gong's washhouse was on the edge of town. Not so far out that people wouldn't want to use the services offered, but far enough to keep the Chinaman and his family out of way of the town proper. When Brawner and Darcy rode up, Gong's wife Chen was busily working a dollystick into a tub full of clothes as though she were churning butter. The sound of the horses made her look up, and she demurely bowed before calling Gong's name over her shoulder.

Three dirty-faced children poked their heads out of the house and cried out with glee when they saw Brawner. "Marsha' Brawner!"

He dismounted as they ran toward him, dropping the reins just in time to catch the smallest and swing him up into the air. "Heya, Hang!" Brawner said.

The children broke into laughter. *"Hang!"* they all corrected him.

"Go! Go!" Gong appeared from the side of the building and shooed the children away. When they were gone, he turned back to Brawner and Darcy. "I wondered if you would come today."

Brawner frowned. "You were expecting us?" He looked at Darcy, bemused, and then his face darkened. The reason for his visit had slipped from his mind again.

Darcy, seeing Brawner's reaction, suddenly seemed to become aware of why he was there as well. He dismounted and stood with the other two men.

"What do you remember, Gong?" Brawner asked.

"Nothing." Gong shook his head. "I remember going into the house, and then…Chen was asking me if I needed tea. She said I had been sitting in the chair, in the dark, for over an hour. Not moving. Not going to bed. She said it scared her."

"Yeah, well, it scares me, too," Darcy said.

"I did about the same thing last night," Brawner said. "I don't remember leaving the ranch. I don't remember going up to the clearing."

"We're going back, aren't we?" Darcy asked.

Brawner looked from Darcy to Gong and then back again, noting the grim looks on their faces. "Do we have a choice?"

"No," Gong answered. "We do not. There is something bad there, and we cannot let it stay."

They looked at each other until the silence became uncomfortable. "No time like the present," Brawner finally said. "Especially as seeing how I somehow keep getting distracted from it."

The sounds of yelling caught their attention, and they all looked back toward town. Two hundred yards on, Brawner spotted two women on the wooden sidewalk in front of the general store. The blonde one held a handgun pointed at the smaller, rounder brunette and was waving it angrily.

"Shit, Goldie," Brawner muttered. He quickly climbed into the saddle and urged his horse towards the two women. Before he could get there, a bolt of red lightning shot across the sky and took Goldie in the chest.

Brawner could see daylight through the hole it left.

Goldie reflexively pulled the trigger on her pistol, and a blue cloud of smoke erupted from it. Annabelle staggered backward, mirroring Goldie's own drunken movements, and the two women fell.

Revolver drawn, Brawner spun his horse to look up to where the glowing red beam of death had come from, to the only place it could have come from—the church bell tower.

He spotted the face in one of the small windows of the belfry just as it ducked out of sight. His blood ran cold. He'd seen that flat gray face and big black lidless eyes before—at the Buescher ranch.

His chest tightened. His throat constricted, and the gun in his hand seemed to weigh a thousand pounds as he tried to raise and point it.

Behind him, Brawner heard Darcy yell out with a deep, throaty roar of unbridled fear and hate. Shots were fired and bullets struck the bell and splintered the wood of the steeple.

"Not this time you bastard!" Darcy screamed, firing and cranking the lever until the repeating rifle ran out.

Brawner's horse reared in fear of the sheer fury of the raging man, throwing the still-stunned marshal to the earth, clutching his gun with a death grip. He hit with a thud that shook him to the bone, but he never took his eyes from the church.

His fear ran as deep as Darcy's as he remembered fragments of what had happened at the Buescher ranch the night before. Strange lights. Smooth, round metal house. Little men who weren't men.

He'd been tortured by them!

A roar of rage, echoing Darcy's, rose in his throat, and he bellowed uncontrollably as he rose to his feet and ran towards the church, revolver held out ahead of him like a bayonet. A shadow moved, and he emptied his gun at it, hitting nothing.

The hammer of Brawner's pistol fell repeatedly, clicking impotently as he continued slamming his palm against it, trying to fire rounds it no longer held. When he realized it was empty, he stopped running, swaying at the foot of the porch to the church.

The shadow moved again. The little gray man, who wasn't a man, seemed to step out of the shadow itself, not ten feet from him. It bared its teeth at Brawner in a hideous grin of its grotesquely small mouth, and Brawner knew it was laughing at him, laughing at what it had done to him last night, at what it would do to him now.

Brawner threw his useless pistol at its oversized head. It leaned to the side, easily dodging the gun, and made a hissing noise as it raised a spindly arm holding a strange silver object and pointed it at Brawner.

There was an explosive noise, and Brawner gasped as a small black spot appeared between the gray thing's big black eyes. It froze in place, unnaturally still, like a fence post, and didn't move. It's shiny suit, made of a fabric that looked like polished silver, glowed with a golden aura.

Chest heaving, Brawner stared at the figure for a moment before stepping forward to take the silver object from its cold fingers. He felt a strange, tingling resistance as he reached for the object, but found if he moved his hand slowly, he was able to go past it. The gray creature's skin felt like that of a snake, cold and smooth, and its fingers were reluctant to release the object.

Brawner's eyes locked onto the large black eyes of the diminutive being, and he realized the black spot between its eyes wasn't a bullet hole—it was a bullet, stopped in midair, barely touching the smooth gray skin of its forehead.

Being so near the pale inhuman monster made Brawner want to vomit, but he worked at the device in its hands until it came free, fitting into Brawner's hand like a toy gun.

He stepped back and glanced over his shoulder to see Gong frantically reloading a long rifle; smoke still drifted in the air around his head. Darcy was on the ground, picking up dropped cartridges for Buescher's repeater. It took only seconds for both men to reload their weapons. Darcy was the first to fire again.

Bullets ricocheted off the motionless creature, sending Brawner scrambling back. When Darcy realized the shots were having no effect, he roared and charged forward, raising Buescher's rifle over his head. The stock splintered and broke in half as Darcy slammed it down over the gray man's head.

The immobile creature remained unaffected.

Brawner looked at the strange thing he'd taken from the monster. He was sure it was the source of the red lightning, a gun of some sort. He raised it and pointed it at the gray thing that wasn't a man.

"Get back!" he told Darcy.

Darcy looked at him, wild-eyed, and then stumbled backwards, away from the creature.

Brawner felt nothing that resembled a trigger so he decided to squeeze and push on every bump he could.

But he couldn't.

Suddenly, he stood frozen as the horrible creature in front of him. The world stilled like a living portrait. The whisper of the soft breeze teased his hair and pulled at his clothes, but the people around him made no more sounds and nothing living moved.

A ghostly shadow, like a shimmering heatwave, appeared in front of him.

Terror pounded up in Brawner's chest. This is what had happened at the Buescher ranch. It was happening again! He struggled, desperately trying to move, but only his eyes, his breathing, and his pounding heart gave evidence they were anything other than stone.

Another gray man stepped out of the strange shadow. But for a strange insignia on the shoulder of its silver suit, it was indistinguishable from the first. It looked from the frozen gray man to Darcy, who was also unmoving, and then to Brawner. And then to the object in Brawner's hand. It approached Brawner slowly, looking into his eyes with its oversized, unblinking black eyes that reflected the world around it like obsidian mirrors.

Reaching out, it plucked the object from Brawner's hand. It grimaced at him, much as the first had, and then raised a long, thin finger and waggled it in front of Brawner's face. Turning away, it walked down the street with a willowy grace until it reached the two women lying on the sidewalk.

At the edge of where he could see, Brawner followed its movements with horror as the gray man bent over Annabelle and waved a glowing red knife over her swollen belly, opening her up like a fish. It reached into her and pulled out her baby, wiping the blood off the infant's face with the skirt of her dress.

The creature stood and walked back with slow deliberation, carrying the infant cradled in one arm. It passed by Brawner and Darcy and went back up to the frozen gray man. Casually, it plucked the bullet from between the eyes of the other and dropped the lead piece on the ground. The red lightning gun seemed to magically appear in its hand, and it tapped the other gray creature on the shoulder with it.

The first gray man stumbled, nearly falling, and then stood up straight and barked at the one holding the infant. With a growl, the newly freed creature turned towards Brawner, Darcy, and Gong. Its eyes were as unnatural as ever, but Brawner recognized the anger and hate in the creature's snarl as it started for him.

The gray man with the insignia barked a word that no human throat could have repeated and raised the gun, pointing it at the now mobile gray man, as if to use it.

The other stopped its charge toward Brawner. It looked at him and snarled before reluctantly turning away and vanishing into a shimmering shadow that had appeared behind it.

Lowering the gun, the inhuman gray being carrying the child stepped forward and followed the first into the shimmer, disappearing before Brawner's eyes. But not before Brawner got a good look at Annabelle's baby—and its oversized black eyes.

It was a triple funeral, and Father Crane took every opportunity to decry the horrors caused by the sin of adultery. A three-way murder of passion, the paper reported, but no one seemed to know much about what happened, other than it was terrible. Within a week, no one seemed to remember anything about it all.

No one except Brawner, Darcy, and Gong.

They each knew, by the haunted look in the others' eyes, that they all remembered. But they didn't speak of it. What was there to say? What was to be done about it?

Nothing. Nothing at all.

Sometimes, at night, on the porch, Brawner found lighting his pipe would put him in a panic that left him cradling his gun until dawn. And sometimes, on the hottest days of summer, he'd find himself drawing his gun at heat shimmers. And sometimes, when he awoke in a cold sweat from nightmares about being tortured and smote by red lightning, he would, just for a moment, see a grimacing gray face snarling down at him.

# Switzerland
## 1848

Hershel straightened up and wiped red paint from his hands onto his apron. The blue paint was already dried to his fingers and didn't come off. He looked at his workbench with a satisfied smile. Everyone had told him he couldn't get the work done in time, but he had refused to give up, and now he had proven them wrong. He had made it.

The one hundredth toy soldier was finished. Nearly two feet tall, it stood proudly in its blue, white, and red uniform, lined up next to the last nineteen he had finished. They all waited, drying at attention. Each soldier was a masterpiece of craftsmanship unlike any toy seen before. Hershel had designed them with a combination of other people's ingenious ideas.

He had learned how to make self-winding mechanisms from Abraham-Louis Perrelet, allowing the soldiers to be wound up merely by shaking them up and down, and, to a lesser extent, self-wind with their own motion. He certainly had not made a perpetual motion machine, but once started, the soldiers could keep themselves going longer than anything else he had ever heard of. It had been quite the challenge to make the soldiers light enough a child, not much larger than the soldier itself, could pick it up and shake it to wind it.

He had used Henri Maillardet's cam memory technology, similar to the gears of a music box, to program the soldiers to march, turn, salute, and present arms. Hershel's favorite part though, was an idea he had gotten from Johann Bohnenberger's apparatus. A rotating sphere, the apparatus' motion kept the soldiers upright as they marched, even across rough terrain such as children are wont to play on.

Hershel had come up with the idea of making one soldier and then using it as a template for all the parts he needed to create the rest. Using a simple machine press, he had punched out identical gears, armor, hats, bayonets…everything. Each soldier was exactly the same, except for the paint job.

The Bürgermeister and the town council will be pleased, Hershel thought as he pulled the paint-stained apron off over his head. It would reflect well upon their province to provide the toy soldiers as Christmas gifts to the entire country in celebration of the Federation established under Switzerland's new constitution. The soldiers were to be used in the Samichlaus Parade as a proud symbol of solidarity, ingenuity, and patriotism. Afterwards, they would be auctioned off to raise money for the orphans and widows left from the *Sonderbundskrieg*, the civil war that had initiated the new Federation.

Hershel had completed them with no time to spare. The shipment would need to go out on the morrow in order to reach Bern, the new capital, in time for the parade.

He realized he had not emptied his bladder for several hours, and an urgency came upon him. He hurried to the door and gasped as he opened it, revealing a chest-high drift of snow, molded with the door's impression.

"Oh, my." Snow was still falling, adding to the barrier in front of his doorway. Looking out into the yard over the top of nature's blockade, he saw snow at least two feet deep everywhere. It was even deeper where the wind dumped the flakes on the leeward side of the trees.

His heart sank. There was no way he could get the toy soldiers into town in time with this kind of weather. The town was nearly ten miles away, and the caravan of sleighs leaving to Bern was set to leave early in the day.

He shut the door, fitting it back to the formed snow drift, and turned to look at the row of soldiers waiting patiently on his work bench. They seemed hopeful, expectant.

Hershel's gaze moved to the crates stacked in the corner of

his workroom where eighty more soldiers lay packed, two in a crate, ready to be delivered. He could visualize them in their slumber, as if resting in their barracks, waiting to be called upon to perform their duty for jubilant children who would likely never see them now.

If they didn't get delivered in time, they would be forgotten and unwanted by next year. The Bürgermeister would never pay freight for them to arrive late. Likely he wouldn't provide payment to Hershel, either. And everyone would say the town council had been right, that Hershel couldn't deliver on his promise.

Hershel sat on his simple wooden stool next to the fireplace and held his tired old face in his hands. A tight knot formed in his belly. He had not only invested everything he had in the soldiers, he had borrowed all of the metals needed to make the soldiers, calling in favors on his good name and the promises of future payments. He would have nothing left. He would be a pauper—and everyone would laugh at him for it.

His bladder finally roused him from his misery. He quickly donned his winter garb and re-opened the door to the snow. With a deep breath, he forced his way through the winter barrier, crawling over the larger part of the drift and reaching back to pull the door shut behind him.

As he headed for the outbuilding, pushing his feet through the heavy drifts, he became resolute. The Bürgermeister and the town council hadn't thought Hershel could make the soldiers in time, but he had, because he hadn't given up. He could clearly remember the jeering muttering of the town's people at the meeting when he had asked to be allowed to make the soldiers, and he didn't like it. He couldn't give up now. He would deliver the toy soldiers. If they didn't arrive in Bern on time, it *could not* be his fault, even if that meant he had to leave tonight.

After relieving himself, Hershel fought through the snow to the barn. He struggled a moment against another snowdrift that had built up in front of the barn doors and let himself in. The horses nickered a greeting at him, and he stopped to rub each of their noses before taking the snow shovel down off the nails that held it to the wall.

Heading back out into the snow, he began shoveling a path

back to his door. He would need to have the way clear in order to load up the crates of soldiers.

Making a path to the barn was hard work with the blowing snow trying to fill in the miniature chasm even as he made it. Packing up the last twenty soldiers and loading all of the crates onto his sleigh took even longer. Every time he carried a crate out to the barn, he couldn't help but count how many more trips he would have to make. As light as he had made the soldiers, they were still heavy when crated, and fifty trips between the house and the barn were more than he thought he had ever made in one day in his life—but the thought of jeering voices pushed him on.

The horses were not pleased about being harnessed, but they were compliant. Hershel wondered if they knew it would be a hard trip by the way he had overloaded the sleigh with crates stacked as high as he could reach and tie down.

It was nearly dark by the time he was ready to leave. The snow had continued to fall, but had not gotten any deeper. Hershel estimated he would be leaving fourteen hours earlier than he had originally planned on. He hoped that would be enough.

He lit the guide lanterns on each side of the sleigh and tucked himself onto the driver's bench with extra blankets to guard against the coming winter night. With a click of his tongue and a flick of the reins, Hershel guided the sleigh out into the snow.

Heavy flakes flew into Hershel's eyes as the horses picked up speed, high stepping in the snow. The sled's runners sank deep with all of the weight, but they glided along smoothly.

With a deep breath, Hershel willed himself to relax and hoped for the knot in his stomach to disappear. He would make it to town in plenty of time. He probably could have waited until morning, but he knew he would have fretted all night and been unable to sleep. He would be able to show everyone what he had accomplished, that they had been wrong about him.

As the dusk faded into night, Hershel had to slow the horses. In many places the trees thinned out enough that, in the dark, he had a difficult time making out where the road actually was. The extra weight on the runners pushed them deeper into the snow than they should have gone, and a few times the sleigh bounced up and down hard as it ran over a large rock, a stump, or a log hidden in the snow, alerting Hershel he had wandered off the road.

The night grew long and cold. Hershel bundled up in the blankets, keeping only his eyes uncovered. The wind and snow bit at his eyelids and soon he had a hard time keeping his eyes open. More and more he relied upon the horses to find their own way, until finally he nodded off.

Hershel awoke in a panic.

His world turned upside down as he was thrown from his seat and a *crack* echoed through the woods. The sled landed on its side next to him, just missing his legs. The lantern on the downside shattered and was extinguished immediately, the other guttered before going out, lasting just long enough for Hershel to see his horses disappearing into the night, giving panicked whinnies as they fled.

And then Hershel was alone in the dark.

The storm's cloud cover was too thick for any moonlight to penetrate. His own ragged breath seemed to fill the night around him as he tried to assess his situation.

He knew he had dozed off. He suspected the horses had egged one another on and picked up speed until they were going too fast for the weather. They must have gone off the road again and hit something, tipping the sleigh.

In the dark, he could hear whirring noises. The sounds were out of place in the silent forest.

He fumbled in his coat pockets until he found matches, and then felt his way around the tipped sleigh in the dark.

Finding the lantern that hadn't been smashed, he re-lit it and discovered the crates holding the soldiers had spilled out into the snow. One had broken open, and the soldiers inside were trying to march, their spring mechanisms having been partially wound by the jolting and their motion-release levers having been tripped by the impact. Hershel picked each one up, flipping their levers and turning them off, and turning them over looking for damage. He had packed them well, and the snow had cushioned the landing. There was not a scratch on them.

He went back to examine the sled. The long wooden shafts

holding the horses to the sleigh had snapped and broken off, unable to bear the strain of the torque caused by tipping. He was grateful the horses hadn't seemed injured. That kind of an accident could have killed them. Or him, for that matter.

It was an easy enough job for Hershel to right the now-empty sleigh, but without horses, he wasn't going anywhere. He unhooked the one good lantern and walked in the direction the horses had gone, calling after them, but he heard nothing and they didn't return.

Disheartened, he headed back to the sleigh and the warm blankets he would need if he were to survive the rest of the winter night.

He had been so close to showing everyone what he had done.

As the dawn broke, Hershel woke, colder than he had been all night. He shook the snow that had accumulated from his blankets as he roused and assessed his predicament.

He sighed deeply. The newer, wetter snowflakes had packed the earlier snow down to a manageable level. If he had only waited until this morning to leave, he would not have had any problems.

He recognized where he was. He could walk into town within a couple of hours, but without the horses, the sleigh wasn't going anywhere. And without the sleigh, he couldn't bring the toy soldiers. It would be too late by the time he could return with help.

Despondent, he began re-loading the unbroken crates, grateful for having packed them well. He was sure they would still be undamaged. Perhaps he would be able to sell them somewhere else. When the last one was replaced, he turned his attention to the crate that had opened.

Hershel packed the first one back in the crate, and then found himself staring at the second one as he held it in his hands. He had come so close…

He flipped the lever to re-activate the soldier, and sadly imagined what the townsfolk might have said when they saw it.

With a hum, the internal gyroscope spun up, making it difficult for Hershel to turn the toy soldier in the air. The soldier smartly saluted him and began attempting to march, lifting its legs high in the fashion Hershel had designed to maximize the effect of the self-winding mechanism.

It reminded him of the way the horses had high-stepped out into the snow last night.

Hershel paused as he considered that. *No*, he shook his head at himself. *What a ridiculous thought.*

Then again, the toy soldiers would not make it to town on time otherwise. He hadn't gotten this far by giving up!

He put the soldier down in the snow to see how it would do. Its head came just above Hershel's knee as it began raising its legs to step high and stomp forward. Its gait was stilted, and it listed slightly from side to side as snow compacted unevenly underneath its feet, but the gyroscope kept it upright, and it moved forward at a steady pace through the snow.

*It could be done!* Hershel grinned wildly to himself.

He shut off the soldier and ran back to dig into the supply box at the back of the sleigh. He came out with a large spool of twine he had used in the past to tie down covers on loads. He tied the twine around the soldier's waist. Grabbing the next soldier, he shook it to wind it, and tied the twine around its waist, connecting the two soldiers. He then turned them on to see how well they did when tied together.

The restricted movement didn't bother their gyroscopes in the least. In fact, Hershel discovered he could easily steer them using the twine as reins.

He briefly considered tying the soldiers to the sleigh, but they had nowhere near the strength needed to move anything but themselves. It didn't matter. This would work. He would get the toy soldiers there on time!

The children were the first to spot the phalanx of one hundred, two-foot tall, toy soldiers marching upon their town. The crisp and bright blue, white, and red colors of the soldiers were sharp against the white snow in the early morning.

Laughing and cheering, the children came and ran circles around Hershel and his troops, imitating the soldier's movements and shouting questions. Hershel steered the column though the snow with relative ease, pulling on the makeshift reins gently enough to make the leading soldiers change course without losing balance.

The joy of the children was infectious, and soon the entire town was in the street, marching alongside Hershel and the toy soldiers as they came down the main street. The townspeople's voices and exuberance filled Hershel's ears and buoyed his spirit.

Everyone shouted questions to him at once: What was all of this? Are they alive? Where are you going? Did you make them?

Hershel laughed and answered as best as he could.

By the time he arrived at the town center, the Bürgermeister was walking alongside him, grinning from ear to ear and taking as much credit as he could.

"Well done," he congratulated Hershel with a slap on the back. "Well done! This will put our town in the forefront of the celebrations for sure!"

Hershel smiled back at him and realized there were several faces from the town council marching alongside as well. They were smiling and laughing, too.

Hershel felt the knot inside of his belly finally let loose and disappear. He had done it. He hadn't given up, and he had finally shown everyone what he could do.

## Kansas

## 1867

I got another one!"

The young Russian woman's accent thrilled Tommy as he watched black powder smoke curl around her delicately arranged black hair.

The train they rode in, the Kansas Pacific Railroad out of Fort Hays headed for Denver, continued to slow as passengers fired out open windows at the racing buffalo herd. Tommy thought the lace finery Miss Veronika wore, and the extravagant red velvet bench seat she knelt one bent knee upon, to be at stark odds with the rifle in her hands and the fierce grin on her face.

The contradiction excited him. He had never met a woman so exotic. She was so cultured, yet so…wild.

"Hoo-Ya!" Baron Avram Alexandrovich, Veronika's father, roared over the sound of the train, the volley of gunfire, and the thunder of the buffalo herd outside. He fired his own rifle repeatedly with the glee of a child on Christmas morning.

Expertly, Veronika levered open the trapdoor on the top of the rifle barrel and pulled out the spent black powder cartridge with her fingertips. She sucked air in through her teeth as she dropped the hot metal casing and held her hand out to Tommy. He handed her a freshly opened box of.50 caliber cartridges and admired the smooth proficiency with which she reloaded the Springfield rifle, turned back to the window, and shot again.

The jostling on the train tracks made aiming difficult, but there were so many buffalo it was hard not to hit one. Although

Tommy could see where Veronika was aiming, he couldn't tell which of the massive creatures she fired at.

Cheers rose from somewhere ahead of the baron's private railcar as three more buffalo dropped from the racing herd. Harsh guttural laughter filtered back with the powder smoke drifting through the windows, thicker than the smoke from the steam engine's fire box. The ten Russian soldiers the baron traveled with were apparently enjoying the sport, as well.

Baron Avram fired again. "Forty! I get forty. Was forty? I lose count!" His roaring laughter filled the car. Boisterous, hairy, and barrel chested, he was nearly the opposite of his daughter in every way.

"Forty-two," Marcus corrected. Marcus, Tommy's childhood companion turned business cohort, wore a boyish grin that matched the baron's as he handed a fifth box of ammunition to the big man.

Tommy knew Marcus would rather be shooting instead of just restocking others, but they had been hired as local advisors for the baron and his daughter, and the money was the best they'd earned since setting out on their own. Their fun would have to wait.

Another empty shell clinked to the wooden floorboards as Veronika loaded and fired again.

Shaking his head, a smile slid across Tommy's face as he watched her shoot. Actually, this was the most fun he'd had in a long time.

The roar of gunfire lessened and dropped to sporadic reports as the buffalo herd veered away and raced south. Brakes squealed and brought the train to a halt as a last few passengers wasted ammunition on targets now out of range.

"Good God! Never before I run out of rifles to shoot because all too hot!" Baron Avram's face was ruddy with excitement as he held his rifle out in front of himself, carefully touching only the wooden stock. Marcus still held one of the other two the baron had been using, having been ready to trade it out again just before the herd turned away.

Tommy took Veronika's rifle as she stepped off the seat she had been kneeling on.

"Now what?" she asked, eyes sparkling with enthusiasm.

"The train will stay here for about an hour while the buffalo runners collect skins and tongues," Tommy said.

A dozen men were already visible through the windows, walking through the prairie grass with knives out.

"Papa?" Veronika's soft brown eyes nearly melted Tommy, even though they weren't aimed at him.

"*Da, da, da.* We go too!" The baron nodded to Tommy and Marcus before stopping and looking down at his resplendent military uniform. "Ah!" He stopped and pointed at Veronika. "Change clothes!"

Veronika looked down at her elaborate dress and pouted her lips but disappeared into her private room as Baron Avram hurried into his own.

Marcus and Tommy, in their worn ranch clothes, looked each other over.

"This is all I got to wear," Marcus said. "You?"

Tommy punched him in the arm.

Blood stained the baron's arms up to his rolled sleeves as he worked his knife around the carcass of the two-thousand-pound bull. Wearing simple pants and white shirt, the supple leather satchel on his hip, with an elaborately stylized emblem of a rearing bear, was the only indication of the uniform he had worn earlier. After a skinner named Riggs demonstrated how, the baron had been eager to help. His boisterous laugh and enthusiasm made quick friends of all the men as Marcus and Tommy held and turned carcasses for him to skin. The knife the baron used, easily twice the size of everyone else's, was the center of the afternoon's jokes.

Until Veronika arrived.

Separating from the crowd of idling passengers, Veronika strode confidently through the grass wearing knee-high boots and wash-leather riding pants. A satchel, matching her father's, rode low on one hip and was the only thing breaking up her womanly outline. She brought many of the men, including the baron's own, to a complete standstill as they watched her pass.

Tommy flushed at his own thoughts, and those he suspected were in the other men's minds. Unable to do anything about the other men, he tore his own eyes away from her figure and forced himself to look at the train instead.

Unmoving, it sat on the tracks as waves of the golden sea of grass splashed around it in the light breeze. A wispy white puff escaped the smokestack at the front while the baron's private car, lacquered black with polished brass trim, was at the opposite end of the train. A dust devil kicked up and swirled chaff around, following the path the buffalo herd had cut through the plains.

"Do you have a knife I could borrow?"

Veronika's unexpected voice at his side made Tommy jump. Her brown eyes, meeting his, looking only at him, stole any possible words from his mouth.

"Everyone else seems to be using theirs." The corner of her mouth pulled up as Tommy looked to see most of the men still standing dumbstruck, watching her.

Swallowing hard, Tommy glanced to Baron Avram.

"Give her knife," the baron grunted, still pulling at the bull's hide. "She can use."

Drawing his knife from its sheath, Tommy handed it to Veronika.

"Do you know how to skin a buffalo?" she asked.

"Yeah." He nodded. "I mean, yes, Miss Veronika."

"Good. Let's start on that one." She pointed with the knife. "Show me how."

"None of the meats?" Baron Avram's voice boomed off the side of the train.

Marcus shook his head, taken aback by the Russian's intensity.

"What is it, Papa?" Veronika asked as she and Tommy approached, both bloody to their elbows.

Avram waved his arms expansively. "They leave all this meats to waste! All!"

"Too much to eat before it would all go bad anyway," Riggs, carrying a bucket full of tongues, said as he passed by on his way to the train.

"There's a bounty on the hides and the tongues," Tommy said. "A lot of men make a good livin' off the buffalo."

The train whistle drowned out the baron's response, but the expression on his face was more than enough for Tommy to decide not to ask him to repeat his words.

"Train leaves in five minutes!" the conductor, walking the length of the train, called out while ringing a hand bell. "All aboard!"

Avram snorted and stalked off toward his men, who had gathered in a small group beside the private car. He waved his arms and shouted in Russian. The harsh guttural language made it impossible for Tommy to guess the baron's temperament, let alone the meaning of the words.

"Don't mind Papa," Veronika assured Marcus and Tommy. "You two are doing a wonderful job." She rubbed her nose with the back of her hand but left a bloody smear on her face anyway.

"Oh, here." Tommy pulled out his handkerchief and offered it. When he saw how gray and dingy it was, he regretted the decision, but it was too late to take it back. She probably had beautifully white lace ones in her satchel.

Veronika took it, wiped at her nose, and gave it back. "You are sweet," she said. "Thank you."

The train whistle blew again.

"We should board now," Veronika said and headed for the train.

"You are sweet," Marcus whispered in Tommy's ear, imitating Veronika's accent.

Tommy punched him in the arm and followed Veronika.

"Grab your bags, boys!" Baron Avram's bellow startled them both. He strutted back from the front of the train with a big grin on his face and his men in tow. "We stay and feast!"

At least twenty men more than the baron's contingent chose to stay and make camp, which surprised Tommy. It would be nearly five days before the train would return to pick them up, and most, like Tommy and Marcus, had little more than the clothes on their backs. Fortunately, Baron Avram had supplies enough to go around.

His men unloaded horses, supplies, rifles, and ammunition with the thought the baron would hunt a buffalo from horseback and take the trophy back to be mounted. Riggs unloaded a stack of wooden crates to be broken down into firewood, while others cleared away grass to make camp and prevent a prairie fire.

While Avram and a couple of men began quartering a large cow, his soldiers set up their tents in neat rows, and Veronika directed Tommy and Marcus in setting up a large, round tent she called a *yurta*.

"Buffalo cider?" Baron Avram's voice carried across the makeshift camp. "Ha! Is joke!"

"What is cider?" Veronika asked as she fastened ties to a pole Marcus and Tommy held overhead.

"Fermented apple juice," Tommy answered.

"Apples?" Veronika wrinkled her nose. "Buffalo apples? Like horse apples?"

Tommy realized she thought buffalo cider was liquid from buffalo droppings and laughed. "No. Almost as bad, but no. It's water in a buffalo's stomach."

"It can save your life out here where there's no other water," Marcus added.

"If you can stomach it." Tommy's face mirrored the disgust on Veronika's as she nearly came nose to nose with him while tying the next cord.

She stopped, arms overhead with fingers lightly touching his hand as he held the pole up and met his gaze.

Tommy's gut tightened and his breath caught. Looking into her brown eyes, inches from his own, he felt a need to protect her, care for her, unlike anything he had ever experienced before. He wanted to sweep her up into his arms and—

A sputtering, choking sound, followed by raucous laughter filled the camp.

"I think the baron must have tried the cider," Marcus said.

Veronika smiled, her face wavering close to Tommy's, then she pulled away and began working the next tie. "That would be Papa."

The grassland took on a fuzzy amber halo as the sun neared the horizon. The rich smell of meat cooked with sage filled the air. Baron Avram supplied vodka. Men, stuffed with meat and heady with liquor, laughed and broke into groups around smaller campfires. Some took up singing while others started a shooting contest, aiming for a distant mound of prairie dogs.

Tommy was careful not to drink enough vodka to cloud his head. He tried to warn Marcus to do the same, but Riggs egged Marcus on until he had to run off and make friends with a sagebrush, which the baron's men found exceptionally funny.

Surveying the camp, Tommy made sure he knew who Veronika was talking to. Satisfied she was all right, he walked behind the yurta to relieve himself.

"You are good boy." Avram startled Tommy as he approached from the other side of the round structure.

"I have been watching. You are good boy. You keeping good eye on my daughter. I thank you." The baron stood next to him and began to make water.

Tommy nodded awkwardly and looked out at the plains until he finished. Buttoning up, he turned back to camp.

"Wait," Avram said.

Hesitating, Tommy looked back to the horizon and waited.

"I see way my daughter looks at you." The baron buttoned up and faced Tommy. "Is good, but is bad at same time. I always want to see her happy, but she is…" he waved his hand as he stumbled over the word, "betrothed."

Avram took in a deep breath through his nose and sighed. "I want you take this." He held out a small leather coin purse.

Tommy reached out and took it. It was deceptively heavy.

"Hide it. Show no one. Is gold. Is payment. You watch my daughter, protect her like I see you want to, but protect her from you, too, eh?" Avram winked. "You are good boy. Many men here. Many maybe not so good as you." He patted Tommy on the shoulder and walked back around the yurta to the camp.

The smell of burnt coffee roused Tommy. Next to him, curled up like a pillbug, Marcus snored lightly.

Tommy punched him in the arm.

"What?" Marcus sat up, looking around wild-eyed.

"Thought you was going to stay awake."

Rubbing the sleep out of his eyes, Marcus winced. "Yeah. Me too."

Commotion at the edge of the camp caught their attention, and they both rose to see. Men were gathering and pointing south, their voices growing louder with excitement. Stepping around the yurta, Tommy and Marcus peered out into the grasslands gilded by the morning light.

Distant shapes moved on the horizon.

"Indians." The word floated over from the crowd of gawkers just as Tommy realized he was looking at five men on horseback.

The watching men chattered nervously.

"That's the Smokey Hill Trail, ain't it?" one of them asked.

"I heard they attacked a stage out there. Killed all the menfolk in the middle of the night," a thin man with bloodshot eyes said. Tommy thought he looked to still be drunk.

"Reckon they on the warpath again?" someone else asked.

"I say we go give 'em a what-for!" the thin man hollered, stepping up to the front of the group, rifle in hand.

A couple began fidgeting with their rifles. The Russian soldiers, curious about the Indians, joined the group.

"Settle down, Martin!" Riggs shooed the drunken man back with his hat. "They ain't no threat. I recognize the tribe. Them's Shawnee. They just followin' the buffaler."

"Oughtta goddamned get back on their reservation!" Martin said, waving a fist at the distant silhouettes.

There were grunts of agreement, but as the dark shapes disappeared behind the slope of the prairie, the grumbling men broke up. After the night's revelries, no one but Martin seemed to feel much like a fight anyway.

"What is all the excitement?" Veronika came out of the yurta wearing the same clothes as the day before, but somehow looking as though she had just bathed and had handmaidens put up her hair.

"Indians," Marcus answered while Tommy gawked at her.

"The native peoples?" She stepped forward to see, but there was no one left in sight.

Marcus shrugged.

Veronika turned and met Tommy's gaze. He realized he was staring and swallowed hard. Feeling the heat on his cheeks, the gold Baron Avram had given him suddenly weighed heavily in his pocket.

"Good morning." Veronika smiled warmly at him.

"Ma'am." Tommy awkwardly half-bowed as he tried to tip his hat.

The distant popping of gunfire reached their ears and the whole encampment turned to look in the direction the Indians had been spotted.

"They are hunting, no?" Baron Avram, coming out of the yurta, called out to Riggs. "We go before they chase buffalo away, yes?"

Tommy had never seen anything quite as tangled and wild as the baron's raised questioning eyebrows.

A breeze with the scent of greenery and fresh water from the nearby Smoky Hill River momentarily pushed the oppressive stench of death away, and Tommy took advantage of it, breathing deeply before the smell came back. The bloody scene they had ridden up on was unlike anything Tommy had ever heard of. Bodies, and parts of bodies, Indian and horse alike, were strewn everywhere. Shredded and ripped to pieces. The carnage was obviously not the work of men.

Looking down from the saddles of their horses, not a single one of the fifteen riders said a word. Only circling flies and nervous horses disturbed the silence.

Veronika coughed into a white-gloved hand, choking on the thick reek that seemed to pool around them.

"I should take you back to camp," Tommy said, but she waved him off. He looked to Avram for guidance, but the baron was already dismounting and looking at the ground.

"*Ya'kwahe...*" a pained, breathy voice called out, startling everyone.

"Here!" Riggs hopped down from his saddle and rushed to an Indian lying crushed under the corpse of a horse with its head torn off.

"*Ya'kwahe.*" The Indian grabbed Riggs' wrist, then mumbled words Tommy couldn't hear.

"Throw me a canteen," Riggs said looking up to the men on horseback around him. Marcus was the first to respond.

Tommy dismounted as Riggs dribbled water into the dying man's mouth. "Let's get the horse off him," Tommy said, trying to decide how to reach around the stump of a neck.

"Don't bother." Riggs reached out his fingers and closed the dead Indian's eyes.

"Many men ask for water when dying," Avram said looking down at the man. "Apparently is thirsty work."

"He weren't askin' for water." Martin, who had come along to 'see what the Injuns was up to', turned his horse sideways so he could watch the nearby tree line. "He was warnin' us about somethin'. You speak his language, Riggs. What's that thing he was talkin' about?"

Riggs stood and brushed off his knees. "An old legend. A giant stiff-legged bear. A fiercely territorial man-eater."

"Bears ain't territorial..." Tommy frowned at Riggs.

"Grizzly done this?" Martin interrupted, laughing nervously and spinning his horse to see behind himself again. "Goddamn big griz..."

One of the Russian soldiers said something and pointed to the ground. Baron Avram hurried over and whistled low.

"This not bear. I know bear, and this not bear. More like… elephant. With claws."

Tommy hurried over to see a round track in the dirt, big enough to put both hands and feet inside.

"Elephant?" Martin cursed. "I didn't head out here with no expectation of seein' the elephant! I'm heading back!" He turned back toward camp and flicked the reins of his horse.

"There are elephants in America?" Veronika asked.

"No," Tommy stepped away from the giant track. "That's just an expression. It means getting into trouble."

A horse scream made them all turn.

At the tree line, Martin was on the ground, rolling away from a furred monster the size of a house.

Bear-like, the creature reared up on hind legs the size of tree trunks but leaned back on a tail just as thick. The creature scooped the horse up into the air with scythe-like claws then fumbled the equine, like a toddling child dropping a doll.

The horse's scream cut short as six-inch claws shredded it from throat to belly, spilling viscera everywhere.

Tommy's riderless horse bolted, followed by the baron's. Everyone started shouting at once. Avram barked orders at his soldiers in Russian, and Riggs remounted, following after the other men spurring their horses to flee.

"Get the baron out of here!" Tommy shouted at Marcus while running to Veronika's horse.

The giant beast dropped to all fours and, despite a strange, stilted gait, moved with amazing speed to capture the fleeing Martin. With a swipe of a paw bigger than Martin's chest, the creature sent the man flying toward Tommy, covering twenty yards in the air before landing and rolling floppily.

Tommy climbed up behind Veronika as the Russian soldiers fired at the charging behemoth. "Go!" he shouted. The other men were already far ahead, racing back to camp.

"Not without Papa!" Veronika fought him for control of the horse, turning back toward the beast.

The volley of fire didn't slow the creature as it charged the group of mounted men that, all together, barely matched its size.

Marcus reined his horse next to Avram and offered a hand. The baron took it just as the soldiers' horses, wild with fear, scattered, tossing men to the ground as the monster arrived.

"Go now!" Avram yelled, dropping back to the ground. He ripped off his shirt and began pulling off his pants. "Go!" He slapped the horse, giving it all the excuse it needed to run away despite Marcus' best efforts.

"Papa, no!" Veronika cried out as she tried to force the horse to her father.

Tommy, forgetting he was trying to take control of Veronika's horse, gaped as Baron Avram pulled a long furry belt from his satchel and wrapped it around his naked waist.

In a heartbeat, the largest brown bear Tommy had ever seen stood in his stead. With a mighty roar, the bear dropped to all fours and charged the giant beast, attacking from the side, distracting it from the men on the ground.

Veronika shoved backwards at Tommy, forcing him to give her room, and then she was off the horse and running toward the battle.

"Veronika!" Tommy tried to go after her, but the horse had had enough and fought to follow all the other fleeing animals. In desperation, Tommy jumped off and, stumbling over part of one of the dead Indians, chased after her on foot.

Peeling her clothes off as her father had, Veronika tripped pulling her pants around her ankles and fell just long enough for Tommy to catch up.

Grabbing her naked arm, he pulled her to her feet. "What the hell are you—?"

"Run away!" Veronika yelled at him as she wrapped a fur belt similar to her father's around her naked body. "Run now!"

Under his hand, her muscles bulged and fur grew. In an instant, Tommy was pushed backward by her bulk and found himself staring up into the eyes of another bear. It roared in his face, teeth grazing his nose, and then it was gone to join the fray.

Stunned, Tommy watched the second, smaller, lighter colored bear run past two Russian soldiers trying to reload their guns while dodging giant swipes of the monster's claws. The other three soldiers were nowhere to be seen. The two bears bit and slashed at the massive beast, pulling back out of reach and then attacking again, worrying at it like hounds.

Then one giant paw caught the smaller bear and sent it rolling through the grass.

"No!" Tommy drew his gun and was running to get to the bear's side before he could think what he was doing. The six shots he fired from his pistol went quick as he tried to distract the monster, but they had no effect. It turned its attention back to the larger bear. Tommy's heart leaped as he saw the smaller bear get back up. He grimaced when it ran back to the fight instead of fleeing.

Knowing it would take too long to reload and prime his black powder pistol, he dropped it and scooped up one of the soldier's rifles. Searching for cartridges, he found two and looked up again just in time to see the tip of an enormous claw gut the last soldier.

Tommy loaded the rifle, fired blindly at the beast, reloaded and fired again. Neither shot seemed to do any damage, but the two bears had managed to carve long bloody rents in the monster's fur. Frantically searching for more unspent cartridges, he began turning over mutilated soldiers and checking pockets.

Something giant and heavy landed next to him. It was the larger brown bear, apparently thrown. It began changing back to the unmistakable pink of a human form.

And the behemoth, now only dealing with one adversary, had its full attention on the smaller bear.

The baron was unconscious, or dead. The furred belt, unbound, lie under him. A squeal of pain from the smaller bear made up Tommy's mind.

Pulling off his shirt, Tommy rolled the baron off the belt and tied it around himself. Instantly, excruciating pain wracked his body. His legs wouldn't work, and he fell to the ground in a terrible agony. Then a tearing, a ripping, and he was free. Powerful. Strong.

He roared with a pure pleasure of strength. Smells overwhelmed him. Blood. Horse. Man. Fear. And Other.

The beast.

Veronika.

He turned to look for her, tripping over the shredded pants clinging to his furred legs. He bit them off easily and charged the monster as it turned in circles to swipe at the light brown bear.

Tommy felt his claws dig into the dirt, giving him traction as he ran. The smell of blood threatened to overwhelm his senses. This combined with his fear for Veronika's safety, sending him into a rage unlike any he had ever known. He was on the beast's back, using his claws to climb the massive monster.

It swatted at him, but Tommy grabbed a mouthful of fur with his powerful jaws and held on like a dog. He caught a good grip and pulled himself higher, nearly reaching the giant neck, and bit again, deeper this time. Blood flowed into his mouth, hot and salty, and with a shake of his powerful head, Tommy tore a giant chunk out.

The monster roared and twisted, trying to dislodge him, but Veronika kept it off balance, attacked its legs, biting at hamstrings. It stumbled, falling to the ground with an earthshaking thump and a thunderous bellow of pain.

Tommy let go and raced away on all fours to avoid being crushed as the beast rolled over to right itself.

With an anguished roar, the creature turned its back to them and ran toward the tree line.

Veronika, racing back to the still form of her father, seemed content to let it go. Knowing he couldn't finish the beast himself, Tommy exhaustedly dropped into a sitting position on his wide haunches and watched it go.

"You are good boy. Very good boy. I like very much." Baron Avram slapped Tommy on the back.

Tommy winced at the sturdy blow that would have hurt even had he not been covered in contusions. He went back to wrapping a clean bandage around the baron's leg. Veronika had helped Tommy scrounge supplies from the saddle bags scattered around and was currently sewing together a pair of replacement pants for him.

"That was not a bear," she said without looking up.

"You think I do not know this?" the baron chuckled.

"Do you remember, in Madrid, the giant skeleton at the *Museo Nacional de Ciencias Naturales*? That was a giant sloth." Veronika used her teeth to break a thread.

The baron nodded. "I think you are correct."

Tommy stood up with a groan. Holding a hand to the purple blotch spreading across his ribs, he said, "Whatever it was, I never want to see it again."

"You know, maybe my daughter is not so…betrothed after all." The baron winked at Tommy. "She would be bear of wife though, da?"

"Papa!" Veronika chided her father as she worked, but her smile was all for Tommy.

The sound of horses made them look up. The remaining Russian soldiers, led by Marcus, came into view, rifles at ready.

"I thought you was dead for sure!" Marcus called out as they approached. He jumped down and ran over to hug Tommy.

Exhausted, Tommy just grinned and hugged him back.

"Where's your pants?" Marcus stepped back and looked Tommy up and down. "Or is that how you chased that thing off?"

Tommy punched Marcus in the shoulder.

# THE SPIRIT OF THE GRIFT

## San Francisco

## 1883

"Spiritualist and Medium," Georges deciphered aloud. The hand-painted sign was decorated with so many flourishes that the storefront name had been rendered nearly illegible. He turned his attention away from the row of businesses lining the street and grinned at his brother Yves. "I believe we have found our next benefactor."

Yves smiled back. "Mother would be proud!" The two looked nothing alike. Georges was dark haired, dark complexioned, and kept himself immaculately groomed, while Yves had a mop of dirty blond hair, grimy fair skin, and teeth that would make a wart-hog jealous.

"You really think so?" Georges looked quizzically at his brother. "I mean, we are kind of cheating…"

"Honestly! Worried about cheating the cheaters? How could you forget the look on Mum's face when she realized she had run out of money, giving it away to swindlers like this?" Yves pointed angrily at the little shop.

"Out the way!" A voice cried out behind them.

Yves and Georges hurried out of the cobblestone street just as an ice wagon raced past. Both brothers gestured rudely at the driver who had not only failed to slow, but had flicked the reins to speed the horses up. The improper gesture befit Yves ragged appearance, but it was comical matched with Georges' pinstriped suit and gentlemanly façade.

"Bastard!" Georges called after the horse and wagon, knowing the insult fell on deaf ears. "I hope your ass freezes to the buckboard!"

"Let it go," Yves patted his brother on the shoulder. Georges could easily work the minor incident up into a major occurrence that would overshadow the next few days. "It's not worth it."

"Still. He's a bastard. Acting like he owns the streets."

"Well, we were just standing in the road gawking like village idiots." Yves's pale countenance went slack-jawed as he made a blank expression at Georges.

Georges reluctantly smiled. "All right, then. Let's go make some money."

"Now yer talkin'," Yves replied in a slurred voice to match his idiot persona. "Oh, wait." He dropped out of character and patted his pockets. "Do you have a kaleidoscope? I don't think I have one on me."

"I've got one. Do you have the ghost-scope?"

Yves rolled his eyes. "I've *always* got that."

"All right then. Again. Let's go make some money."

Georges glanced up and down the street to make sure no more carriages would try to run him over before stepping back out onto the cobblestones. He straightened his jacket cuffs, adjusted his waistcoat, and corrected his posture to be as stiff as possible. He strode across the street with an air of dignity.

Yves followed, slouching and swinging his arms like the hunchback of Norte Dame.

The kingly fashion in which Georges entered the shop was wasted on the unoccupied room. The show Yves put on, attempting to open the door Georges had allowed to shut in his face—by using only the backs of his hands, was also wasted. Neither brother was discouraged in the slightest.

Looking around at the shelves and glass display cabinets full of expensive oils, potpourris, and incense, Georges smiled to himself. This place obviously made plenty of money.

"Ahem!" Georges cleared his throat in the rudest polite way possible.

On the other side of the room, Yves began picking at the seat of his pants with one hand while stretching up on tip-toe to try to reach glass baubles off the top shelf of a display with the other.

When no one emerged from the back, Yves went ahead and knocked a few of the curios off.

The resulting sound of shattering glass quickly summoned two people; an overweight middle aged man wearing standard homemade burlap pants and shirt, and an attractive young woman in a velvety red dress befitting a spiritualist. The man wore a sour look and had a small club clenched tightly in in one fist. The woman, wild-eyed, held the top of her bodice together with one hand while frantically trying to button it up with the other.

Georges had a hard time deciding which of the two he most wanted to keep his eyes upon. Fortunately, Yves chose that moment to curl up on the floor and begin wailing like an infant.

Rolling his eyes up toward the heavens, Georges assumed the look of someone so disaffected he might die just to relieve his boredom. "Oh, puh-lease! Not again. Three times in one day is quite enough!"

Georges spun on his heel and marched over to Yves. "Here." He pulled a telescoping brass tube from his coat pocket and held it out.

Yves peeked through his fingers to see what was being offered before he stopped crying. When he saw the kaleidoscope, Yves snatched at it instantly. Tears a thing of the past, Yves put the tube to his eye and grinned as he looked around the room.

With a heavy sigh, Georges tiredly turned back to the other two people in the room. "I am terribly sorry. I will pay for whatever it is he has broken."

The heavy man's knuckles returned to a normal color as he relaxed his grip on the club. The woman turned her back to Georges and Yves and quickly finished buttoning up the front of her dress.

"I've got it, Papa," she whispered.

The man eyed Georges, then Yves. Yves eyed him back through the kaleidoscope with a silly grin. Grunting, the man returned to the back room.

"Please, sir," the woman called Georges attention back to her, "allow me just a moment to clean up the glass." She bent down behind the sales counter.

As soon as she was out of sight, Yves put the kaleidoscope in his pocket and pulled out an identical looking brass tube, his ghost-scope.

The woman came out from behind the counter with a broom and dustpan and began sweeping up the colored shards from the wooden floor.

Yves followed her every movement with his scope. Georges was hard pressed to keep a straight face as Yves waggled his eyebrows at the young woman's lithe form.

A nearly overwhelming scent of perfumed flowers and fruits filled the air, mixing with a horrid burnt smell.

"Dear God!" Georges covered his nose with the back of his hand. "What is *that*?"

Yves retreated to the farthest corner of the shop and began feigning retching noises. At least Georges thought Yves was pretending.

"I'm terribly sorry, sir!" The woman continued cleaning. "Some of those oils were quite rare and valuable because of their strong scents."

"Hmph!" Georges almost sniffed in disgust, but thought better of it. "*Of course* they were."

With an apologetic smile, the young woman finished sweeping up the shards and took them into the back room. When she returned, she opened windows and used a small wooden stool to prop open the front door.

Yves went back to looking at everything in the shop through his mock-kaleidoscope, although he continued to make quiet gagging noises.

Georges, still holding the back of his hand to his nose, was on the verge of gagging himself. "Perhaps I should return later, after this has aired a bit."

"Oh yes, sir," the woman bowed slightly. "That might be a wise choice."

Georges narrowed his eyes at her. "Are you trying to get rid of me?"

"Oh, no—!"

"Do you find you have difficulty hiding your disdain for my poor brother? Do you think it improper that a wealthy family would keep one if its own around instead of putting him in an asylum or turning him out to the gutter?"

"Sir! I—No!" The woman's face turned red as she became flustered.

"You'll not be rid of me that easily! I came here to speak with the dead, and I'll not leave until I have!"

"Please, sir. This way." She pointed to a wooden door in the back. "We hold our séances back here where the bright of day doesn't interfere as much."

When Georges didn't follow her gesture, she led the way.

"Come, Tomás," Georges said to Yves. "Let us go see if Mummy will talk to you here."

"Mummy!" Yves spoke for the first time since entering the shop. "Mummy, Richie! Mummy!" He jumped up like a child and danced over to hug Georges.

"Yes, Tomás, Mummy." Georges stiffly hugged Yves back for a moment before pushing his brother away again and straightening his jacket.

"Where? Where Mummy?"

"In there, Tomás. In that room. Let's go."

Yves stopped and looked around with a confused look on his face. "No Mummy?" he said to the air. He frowned deeply. "No Mummy!" he told Georges and stomped his foot.

Georges sighed. "Let's go see anyway, Tomás."

"No, Richie! No Mummy!"

"Please, Tomás. Let's go see."

Yves pouted. "Richie. No Mummy."

Georges put his arm around Yves. "Please. For Richie? Come on." He began gently pulling Yves toward the back room.

Georges gave the woman a weak apologetic smile as they crossed the threshold to enter the darkened room. He looked over his shoulder and quietly whispered "Tomás thinks he can talk to an invisible lady named Angelica, and she tells him things. Right now she seems to be telling him we will not be seeing our mother here."

"The spirits do as the spirits wish, sir." The woman seemed to plead with her eyes. "We will see what we can see."

She followed them in and the room went dark as she closed the door. A clicking sound repeated three times as she twisted the key on the wall to light the gas fueled sconce. A warm glow filled the room as the flame came to life and revealed the dark red velvet drapes that hid the walls. Mostly filled by a large round table with a glass ball for a centerpiece, the room also held eight chairs, gathered around the table, and a large portrait of a scowling older woman.

"Please, sit." She gestured to the chairs.

Georges led Yves to a chair and put him in it before sitting himself. The woman took a moment to straighten her dress and her hair, and then, with a flourish, she walked around to the large leather covered chair that established the head of the table.

"I am Madame Limatana, and here, in this room, the spirits do *my* bidding." She waved her arms wide and looked upwards with a distant gaze. Yves followed the pretty young woman's every movement through his kaleidoscope so intently Georges began to worry Yves might break character again.

Madame Limatana seated herself in the leather chair and placed her hands upon the table. She began murmuring a rhythmic chant and swaying in her seat while sliding her hands around on the table.

The light abruptly dimmed. The two men could barely make out the woman's silhouette. Yves made appropriate frightened sounds and leaned into Georges for comfort.

The slight glow from the eye piece of Yves's ghost-scope caught Georges' eye and he quickly put his hand over it. Yves pulled away sharply, as though he thought Georges was going to take Tomás' precious kaleidoscope away from him, but he had gotten the hint and the scope disappeared into his pocket, hiding the faint luminescence.

"Spirits! I sense your presence!" Madame Limatana opened her eyes and looked around the room. "Reveal yourselves to us!"

The glass globe in the center of the table began to glow a faint blue. Madame Limatana reached out and caressed the ball with her hands.

"I see your mother…" Her whispered breathily. "She is not happy. She has been trying to contact you, but something has been stopping her. I can hear her. She is saying…Richie. Richie. Richie." As she whispered the name, it echoed faintly from elsewhere in the room, imitating her tone and cadence. "Richie, why won't…" Madame Limatana's voice faded out as the other voice grew to a whisper.

"…you listen to me? Richie? Your brother needs you to be strong!" The voice seemed to come from above them. It was just loud enough to be heard, but not loud enough to recognize the identity of the speaker.

Madame Limatana's eyes were focused upward.

Georges pretended to look up as well, but kept his eyes upon the young woman.

"Not Mummy," Yves whispered to himself and cradled his kaleidoscope. "Not Mummy."

"Tomás? Can you hear me, dear? Tomás?" The voice faded slightly, making it even more difficult to recognize. "Are you being good for Mummy?"

Georges saw Madame Limatana do something with her hand next to her ear, and he knew she was ready for the next trick. Under the table, he nudged Yves' foot with his own to give his brother warning.

"Are you …" The overhead voice faded.

"…being good for Mummy?" Madam Limatana finished the sentence with her eyes closed. "I need you to be a good boy." The chair Madam Limatana sat in began to slowly rise, taking her up into the air with it. It stopped when her knees reached the height of the tabletop. She shook her head from side to side, as though trying to wake up. "Be good for Mummy! Mummy has to go now. Be good!" She opened her mouth and a ghostly white form began to emerge from within her.

Slowly coming out like smoke, the pale form seemed to expand and rise as it materialized from Madame Limatana's body. Madame Limatana's form undulated eerily slow and fluidly, as though underwater, seemingly trying to wake herself up.

"Not Mummy." Yves voice was quiet, yet carried the shrill edge of panic. "Angie says not Mummy."

"Shhh! Tomás. Everything is all right." Georges whispered.

The last of the ectoplasmic form came out from Madame Limatana's mouth, and her eyes flew wide open as she jerked awake and her chair crashed back down to the floor.

"Angie says not Mummy!" Yves stood up angrily. "Angie says man and woman trick Richie! Angie says fake!" He threw his kaleidoscope through the ghostly apparition floating across the room. The brass tube hit the middle of the suspended cloth, tore a hole through it, and continued on into the curtains covering the walls where it hit with a loud *thud*.

"Yi!" A figure cried out and stumbled out from behind the curtain.

Georges stifled a grin. Yves' marksmanship was good.

"What the hell is going on here?" Georges stood up angrily.

"Papa!" Madame Limatana rushed to check on the man who had held the club earlier.

"You have deceived us!" Georges pointed with a shaking finger.

"Fake!" Yves yelled again and pointed at the glass ball on the table. "Fake!" He pointed at the chair Madame Limatana had been sitting in. "Fake!" He went around the room pointing at things, both seen, such as the scowling portrait, and unseen, such as the curtain he pulled open to reveal a woman who looked just like the portrait.

The woman shrieked and covered her mouth with her hands, unable to decide whether to go help the injured man or try to hide.

"Mama! Papa's hurt!" Madame Limatana called to her.

Georges strode over to the gas light on the wall and turned the key, brightening the room.

"Fake!" Yves tugged on strings that pulled some sort of balloon out from behind another curtain.

Madame Limatana's father finally managed to stand upright. A rivulet of blood ran down his cheek from where the kaleidoscope had struck his eyebrow. "Stop," he called out.

"Fake!" Yves pulled a hidden lever and a wind started up, blowing the curtains and the fake ghost with a rippling effect.

"Stop!" The man roared and stomped toward Yves. "Stop!"

Yves fell into a ball where he was and began sobbing loudly.

"How dare you!" Georges approached the man threateningly. "You charlatan! How dare you try to take advantage of us and then yell at my brother as though *he* has done something wrong!" Georges raised his hand as if to backhand the man.

"Stop. Please stop." Madame Limatana put herself between the two men. "Please."

The older woman ran over and protectively placed herself between Georges and Madame Limatana.

Georges lowered his hand and pulled himself up erect, straightening his coat. "You have not heard the last of me. You will be hearing from my solicitor." He stiffly walked over to where Yves was still crying on the floor.

"Sir, please," Madame Limatana followed him, "allow me the chance to explain."

Georges ignored her. "Come, Tomás. Let us get away from this place. I'm sorry I didn't listen to what you said about Angelica. She was right. I will listen in the future. Come on." He held out his hand.

Yves began reaching up, but stopped, his eyes upon the kaleidoscope he had intentionally stomped upon while yelling 'Fake!' and exposing the rigged props. His mouth dropped open and his eyes went wide as he pointed at the broken toy. His jaw began working, but no sound came out.

Georges followed Yves pointing finger until he was looking at the glass shards and smashed brass tube. He allowed his own countenance to darken into a hopeless despair. "Oh dear God, no."

Yves let loose with a mighty ear shattering wail and began crawling toward the broken toy.

Georges blocked his way. He bent down and scooped the man up like a child, holding his crying countenance into his shoulder. He turned, glaring with burning eyes, and hissed. "That was the only thing he had from our mother. It was the only thing that calmed him."

"Sir, I am so sorry…"

He turned his back to them and carried the sobbing Yves out the front door and into the street.

"God Almighty! How much farther? You weigh as much as a mule," he grunted into Yves ear.

"Go 'round the corner," Yves sobbed into his shoulder as he kept an eye on the store's front door.

Georges made his way between buildings, dropping his brother the instant tapped him to let him know they were out of sight.

"Oh, thank God. My poor back."

"How'd it go?" Yves asked. "Did they look worried?"

"Not as worried as I would have liked, but enough I think. You might have ruined it by scoring the man in the eye!"

"Not like he didn't have it coming. He's back there bilking money from poor old ladies who believe in his malarkey. They're not any better than the people who took all of Mum's money pretending they were talking to Father."

"Let's circle to the back of the building and see if we can figure out what they are up to." Georges suggested.

Yves nodded and pulled his ghost-scope out of his pocket. It looked just like the broken kaleidoscope. As they neared the back of the building, he extended the scope to its full length and began looking through it.

"Anything?" Georges asked.

Yves shook his head and passed the ghost-scope over.

Georges held it to his eye and examined the view of the world it provided.

The back of the building became as if nothing more than a yellowish shadow, revealing other, darker yellow shadows within. Georges could make out three figures moving around, and he could even tell which was Madame Limatana and which were her parents, but was hard to tell what they were doing. The man waved his arms quickly and angrily as the women followed him around the shop, appearing to talk and lay hands upon him to calm him, but beyond the movements of their shadowy outlines, details were lost.

"The walls are too thick." He handed the scope back to Yves. "Did you have any trouble using it inside?"

Yves put the scope in his pocket.

"A little. Not too bad. I could see well enough to find all of their tricks. How long do you think we should wait before we go back?"

"What do you want to try to get? Hush money or part of the business?" Georges' eyes gleamed with excitement.

"I still feel trying to get part of the business will come back to haunt us one of these days. I still think we are better off just taking money and never having anything lead back to us. If someone gets really upset about paying us off every month, they could track us down through a bank deposit."

Georges frowned. "In that case, I say we go back tonight."

"Sir! There you are! Please! You didn't give me the chance to explain!" Madame Limatana had turned the corner and spotted them.

Georges cursed under his breath as Yves quickly pretended to be quietly sobbing.

"Please, come back." The woman hiked the edge of her dress up as she hurried over to them. "Please. I can put this right if you will just give me the chance."

Georges glanced at Yves who was having a hard time hiding a satisfied smirk as the woman closed in on them. Yves nodded slightly.

"And just how do you intend to 'put this right'?" Georges asked.

She stopped and curtsied as she reached them. "I am so sorry about your kaleidoscope," she told Yves, who refused to meet her eyes. "We can see about getting you a new one. Maybe a better one, even."

Turning back to Georges, she bowed slightly again. "Please, sir. Please come back."

Georges sighed exasperatedly. "I will give you five minutes. Come, Tomás."

Yves resisted, shrugging off Georges' hand. "Not Mummy."

"I know. But let's go see what they have to say. Please. For Richie."

Yves reluctantly followed Georges and Madame Limatana back to the shop. He made retching sounds as they walked through the lingering odor of the spilled oils.

Madame Limatana's parents were waiting for them. The man's eyebrow had stopped bleeding, and the blood had been mostly cleaned off his face.

"Sir," began the man, "We are terribly sorry for any distress we may have caused you and your brother. It's just…"

He broke off looking for the right words.

"It's just that you are frauds, bilking good honest people out of their money with your petty lies designed to give them false hope." More bitterness from his own history crept into Georges' voice than he had intended.

"Oh, no sir." Madame Limatana stepped forward again.

"We have found," interjected her mother, "that most people who claim they want to speak with the dead truly do not. They want to feel released of burdens and obligations to the departed, but they rarely want to actually speak with the deceased."

"Which is why we installed our diversions and gimmicks," Papa finished. "To allow us to grant them that peace of mind. But if you truly wish to speak to the spirits of the departed, we can accommodate you." He pointed back to the room Yves had nearly torn apart and eyed Georges challengingly.

Georges hesitated for a moment, but Yves made the decision for him by marching into the room muttering "Fake."

Georges followed. Madame Limatana was the last to enter the room, closing the door behind her parents as they followed Georges.

Mama seated herself at the head of the table where Madame Limatana had been before. Papa and Madame Limatana followed suit, sitting to either side of Mama, who gestured for Georges and Yves to sit as well.

Yves noisily wiped his nose on his sleeve and climbed into a chair, sitting while holding his knees close to his chest. Georges managed an affect of impatience as he seated himself.

"No need to turn off the lights?" he asked snidely.

"No." The old woman's answer was neither terse nor acquiescing. "The spirits care not." She held out her hands to her daughter and husband, and they took hold of them. Papa offered his hand to Georges while Madame Limatana reached for Yves'.

Yves grabbed the young woman's hand with a silly childish grin that Georges thought was likely less than half faked. With a sigh, Georges took Papa's hand and then took hold of Yves other hand, completing the circle.

Mama closed her eyes and bowed her head, muttering a chant. The room began to take on a chill and the gas light fluttered although there was no breeze. Her voice began to take on an ethereal quality, a lilting timbre beyond the capability of a human voice.

"Georges? Georges, is that you?" The voice came from the woman, but seemed to be all around at once. Georges went pale at the sound of his real name.

Yves' eyes went wide and flashed from Georges to the woman leading the séance.

"Oh, my poor, poor little Georges."

As something touched him, Georges jerked upright and pulled his hands back, turning to see behind himself, and feeling the back of his head.

"Yves! For shame!" the voice continued.

Yves nearly fell out of the chair trying to turn around.

"Why do you lead your brother around the country like this? It's not good for either of you. And don't get me started on how you are wasting your father's invention!" The room grew very cold as the ghost scope lifted up out of Yves' pocket and hovered in the air before them.

Yves grabbed at it, but then dropped it on the table, as though he had been burned. Frost rapidly grew like ivy across the brass and filmed the lenses.

"So many good things you could have done with it. You could be helping doctors heal people. You could be letting others see it to learn how to make another. But no. My children use their father's greatest gift to them for petty extortion and cheap thrills with poor unsuspecting women."

Yves face jerked as an audible slapping sound filled the room. His hands flew up to cover his reddening cheek.

"God Almighty!" Georges eyes were wide in fear.

Madame Limatana's hair swirled behind her head as though someone were lovingly stroking it. She was unfazed by the ghostly touch and even gave an appreciative smile to the air above her.

"Lavinia. Boamos." Madame Limatana's parents both looked up. "You do a good thing here. I am sorry my sons have caused you so much trouble. They didn't understand what you do. They will fix everything they broke and pay for everything they can't."

"*Sastimos, Didikai,*" Mama said with a gentle smile.

The wind ruffled Mama's hair and then a cold chill surrounded Yves and Georges. Both of their chairs began to rise into the air and they grabbed the edges for balance.

"Mind your mother, boys," their mother's disembodied voice warned. "Put this right, and get your lives straight before it is too late."

The chairs slammed back to the ground, nearly sending Georges and Yves falling out of them. And then the presence was gone.

Georges' breath came in rapid pants in the silence that followed. Yves scrambled to grab the ghost-scope off the table and held it to his eye, searching desperately for any hidden mechanism that could have lifted his chair.

Madame Limatana and her parents stood up with gentle, yet self-satisfied smiles upon their faces.

"You can start by re-hanging the curtains," Papa told them and left the room, followed by Mama.

"And I'll thank you to never look at me with that scope again." Madame Limatana's cold gaze and tone of voice froze Yves where he was.

Georges shakily got out of his chair and imitated Yves by examining it, but his examination was cursory. "I think that really was Mother," he whispered. "We shouldn't have been doing this. I told you! We were the crooks all along. How many people have we…?"

Yves grabbed Georges' shoulder and spun him. A huge red welt in the shape of a handprint covered his cheek. "If that was really Mother, then why did she slap me for being a Peeping Tom, but not you for blasphemy?"

"I didn't blaspheme!"

"Yes you did." Yves waved his arms angrily. "When I got slapped you yelled out 'God Almighty!'"

A slapping sound filled the room and Yves' head jerked sharply to the side. When he looked back at Georges, he had welts on both sides of his face. He glared at Georges. "Mother always did like you best."

# GOING TO HELL ON THE NOON TRAIN

## Kansas Territory

## 1860

The steady clacking of the train on the rails had just begun to fade into background noise for me when the brakes squealed, throwing me into the back of the next row of seats. Passengers screamed as the train shuddered to a halt, sending luggage and people tail over teakettle toward the front of the car. I might have enjoyed watching the ladies show off their petticoats and ankles had the prisoner handcuffed to my wrist not taken advantage of the moment and punched me in the side of head with his free hand.

Fortunately for me, Max Drane's dominant hand was the one attached to my wrist. Still, he managed to ring my bell, and next thing I knew he was on top of me, rummaging through the pockets of my leather pantsuit, looking for the handcuff key.

"Not nice to touch a lady without her permission, Max," I said, grabbing his wrist with my free hand. "I would have thought you'd have figured that out by now. You know, with the hanging and all."

I received a head-butt in the nose for a reply.

Blood exploded everywhere and my vision began to fade with the pain.

"You ain't no lady!" His breath stunk as he growled in my face. "I don't know what the hell you are!"

Max's hand groped around at my hip, and I knew he was going for my sidearm.

It was time to stop playing around.

I jabbed my index finger into his carotid artery and pressed the side of my center knuckle with my thumb. A needle shot out from under my fingernail and injected a fast acting sedative into his blood stream. Max's eyes were glazing over before I could retract the needle, and the full weight of his smelly, unwashed, nineteenth century body came down on top of me.

"That's the thanks I get for saving your life?" I murmured into his smelly ear.

No matter how I tried, I couldn't get over the way the people here stunk. I don't know which was worse, the reek of his old sour sweat, the fecal smell that occasionally wafted from his burlap pants, or the stench of his infected-tooth breath. Either way, I had a serious need to get out from under him.

Reaching inside my shirt, I took the key out of the hidden pocket sewn into my bra and used it to unlock the manacle that bound me to the noxious bastard. Pushing him off, I left the cuffs dangling from his wrist and rubbed at the bruised ring around my own. He would be out for a good three or four hours, and I saw no reason why he had to be within my personal space during that time.

I didn't need to do much with Max, other than to make sure he didn't interact with anyone now that he was past his Deadline. If anyone knew who he was, now that he was supposed to be dead, it could have serious repercussions within the timeline. The nanos I had injected him with yesterday had altered his facial appearance enough that there was no fear of anyone recognizing him, so now that he was unconscious and couldn't talk, I had little to worry about. I cuffed him to the iron leg of the bench seat and got myself up off of the floor.

The train had come to a full stop sometime during my scuffle and people were gathering themselves up. No one seemed to have noticed my fisticuffs, and I was not the only one with a bloody face. I considered wiping the blood off with Max's shirt, but I couldn't bear the thought of touching the filthy thing to my face. The throbbing in my nose was nearly gone already anyway. The nanos in my own bloodstream were state of the art, and their repair job would be nearly painless and nearly perfect.

I was tempted to cheap shot the bastard while he was out, you know, a nose for a nose, but he would have all of eternity to think about how he had spent his few minutes with me anyway, so I let it slide.

Excited chatter from the people looking out the windows caught my attention, so I stepped up onto the middle of Max's back and leaned out of the boxcar window to see for myself.

The front half of the train had gone into a tunnel.

Of sorts.

What I mean is; the tunnel was there, and the train faded off into the darkness of the tunnel, but the mountain that should have surrounded the tunnel wasn't there.

Not that a mountain was missing, mind you. There were no mountains in the middle of the Great Plains. There shouldn't have been a tunnel either, but, well, there it was, somehow existing without actually being a tunnel into something.

I had seen a holographic projection kind of like it once. It had been a demonstration of a reverse hologram actually, where they were showing how to remove the light from an area rather than adding light to create an image. That's not what this was though. The train inside would have been hidden by the lack of light. The whole thing would have just looked like a black spot. This was really some kind of tunnel.

A wormhole, maybe? The term came unbidden to my mind. It was an old scientific theory that had gone to the wayside long ago. Space travel wasn't really my shtick, so I didn't know much about it other than research had stopped when the use of Time Teleportation solved the problem of traveling faster than light.

I turned away from the window, making sure to grind my boot into Max's back as I spun on my heel, and headed for my luggage.

As a Malefactor Acquisitions Agent for Her Majesty's Time Continuum Exploration, Expansion, and Exploitation Department, I was allowed little in the way of technology when traipsing around in the past. The nanos to heal myself were standard, to protect me from ancient voodoo-type medicines and diseases, but the needle under my nail was pushing it to be quite honest. I was one of the best agents, and I was always willing to take the riskiest assignments, so I had earned a privilege or two, like getting to wear a bra, but nothing that would help me deal with something like this.

Stepping around other people's fallen items, I paused to help up one particularly cute woman who couldn't have been a day over twenty. I gave the nineteenth century gal my most charming smile, wondering what my chances were as I retrieved my smaller bag and dug out my comm. Fraternizing with her was against the rules, but she was pretty enough to be worth it.

The look on her face reminded me that my own face was still covered with blood.

Disappointed, I turned away, put my bag back, and headed for the door with the comm in my hand.

Made to look like a worry stone with one side rubbed smooth, the device fit well with any time period I might be visiting. I pressed my thumb into the worn depression and, recognizing the signature of my nanos, it activated.

A tone, carried by electronic impulses through my nanos and audible only to me, beeped in my ears and indicated a connection.

"TCEEED H.Q." A voice followed the tone, pronouncing the acronym 'seed'. "Agent Barbara Randall please state the nature of your emergency."

"Activate optical," I mumbled, stepping out into the prairie and walking away from the train so that I would be able to look back and take in more of the darkness swallowing it.

"Activating optical," the voice replied, and I knew they could now see what I saw.

"Susan? Is that you?" I asked, recognizing the voice.

"Checking Time Correlation Code." Her response was curt.

It was Susan. I waited a moment for her to determine when in my life this event occurred in relation to when it was occurring for her. Time travel could really muck stuff up, and we had to be careful of ruining our relationship should I be calling in fifteen years later than the next time we would actually meet in person. There were safety protocols to prevent it, but sometimes things went south anyway.

"Hey, Babs!" Susan said, her voice no longer monotone and professional. "TCC is only a month since the last time we saw each other."

"Nice! That means we could still talk about the way you were able to—"

"Didn't you have an emergency?" Susan interrupted me.

"Oh, yeah. Sorry I was distracted by the memory of your—"

"Babs, this is a recorded emergency channel."

I clucked, rejected by a woman for the second time in as many minutes. "Get a load of this," I said, turning and facing the strange sight.

At least half of the train was inside the tunnel of darkness. I could see the passengers of those cars stumbling out and looking around in confusion. No one seemed injured, beyond what I would have expected from our sudden stop. Some were running back out toward the light, while others milled about. A few had dropped to their knees in prayer. One of them was the train's conductor. I rolled my eyes and looked away from the prostrated ignoramuses. Some people find God in anything they don't understand.

No one headed farther into the darkness.

"What are we looking at here, Agent Randall?" A coolly authoritative voice filled my ears. Susan's supervisor must have taken interest.

"I don't know, ma'am." My reply was brief. I couldn't afford any more subordination write-ups, no matter how good my return rate was. "It appears to be a tunnel of some sort, perhaps leading into another time or place?"

"Can you move farther out so we can see more of the outside of the phenomenon?"

"Yes, ma'am." I turned and walked farther away from the train, watching my footing around the prairie dog holes and cactus plants. When I had gone another hundred yards, I turned and looked back again.

The blackness of the tunnel faded out the farther it was from the entrance. Not like dissipating smoke, but more like a superimposed image fading away. In the darkest parts of the tunnel, inside the mouth where the train and the people were, I felt like I could see movement in the dark void. Something blacker than the black, moving around in there, something I shouldn't be able to see, but somehow I almost could…

"Agent Randall, please state the status of your current assignment."

"Currently transporting Malefactor Acquisition Max Drane to pick-up location, for transfer and interment into the Queen's Non-Dimensional Dungeon."

I scratched at the itchy, drying blood on my cheek. Yessir, ol' Max was going to have all the rest of eternity in there to think about how he had treated me. A smile twisted across my lips at the thought.

I don't know that the NDD is really anything like a dungeon at all. You would think I'd know something about it, as it's my job to find the bad guys so they can be sent there, but I don't want to know what the Dungeon really is. It's more than enough to know that it's forever. The Queen reserves it for those picked out by Research as having committed particularly atrocious crimes against humanity. They send me out to capture the baddies just before the time of their Deadline. By replacing them with a tissue clone temporarily animated by nanos, I steal them away and prevent their physical death just long enough to put the bastards into the Queen's Non-Dimensional Dungeon where they can atone for their crimes for the rest of eternity.

"Status of prisoner at this time?" the supervisor asked.

"Unconscious. Handcuffed within the train." I hoped she didn't ask how he came to be unconscious. "I deemed the prisoner to be low priority in the current situation."

The supervisor grunted as though it had not been my call to make but she agreed with the assessment. "Agent Randall, do you feel comfortable approaching the phenomenon?"

"Yes, ma'am," I lied as I looked into the unnatural tunnel. For some reason I couldn't put my finger on, I was feeling afraid for the first time I could remember. Not just nervous or leery, but actually afraid. I never had been afraid of the monster in my closet or the bugaboo under my bed. Hell, I wasn't even afraid when someone like Max pointed a gun at my head. I was used to it.

But something about this was setting me on edge.

"Please do so. Report all observations for the record."

"Yes, ma'am." I hoped the recording didn't catch the slight tremble in my voice.

I strode forward with a confidence I didn't feel.

Approaching the tunnel from a side angle, it appeared as though I was looking at a holographic projection with broken emitters. The more tangential I was to the front of the tunnel, the more it faded out. I aimed my approach to see if I could actually get a glimpse from behind the tunnel.

"From the backside, the tunnel does not seem to exist," I reported aloud for the record being made from my transmission. "Note the strange appearance of the boxcar half within the tunnel formation."

I couldn't take my eyes off it. From this vantage, the train car appeared as though it had been cleanly sliced in two with a monomolecular saw and left as a cross section example in a museum.

"Noted," the supervisor's voice said in my ear. "Images are being forwarded to Research to see if the phenomena can be identified."

A man, coming from where he had been invisible to me, stumbled out of the tunnel, his body magically appearing before me like slices of a living vivisection being recompiled to make him whole again. I've never been squeamish, but seeing his working innards in cross section…

I nearly threw up in my mouth.

A sound over the communications in my ear told me Susan had reacted the same way.

Completely unaware of what I had just seen happen to him, the man walked out into the plains, raising one hand to shield his eyes from the sunlight.

I turned to look behind me. "There is no indication that anything in the tunnel exists within this…frame of reality." I groped for words to describe what I was, or rather wasn't, seeing.

"Noted."

Turning back to face the half-boxcar, I spotted a woman walking hesitantly toward me, peering at me as though she couldn't see well. I realized she wasn't looking at me. She couldn't see me, she was looking into the gloom of the tunnel and considering entering it.

The thought of seeing the insides of her body as she disappeared, the opposite of the way the man had appeared, as though parts of her were being instantly dissolved, made me hurry forward so that I wouldn't have that image burned into my brain for all eternity.

I knew the instant I passed the threshold of the tunnel, because the woman jumped in terror at my sudden appearance. Clutching at her bosom with one hand, she quickly turned around and hurried away in a rustle of petticoats.

"The phenomenon appears to be one way," I said, again searching for words that didn't seem to accurately assess the situation. I watched the woman rejoin a scared group of passengers. She started hyperventilating. Normally I would have blamed it on her silly nineteenth century sensibilities, but I was feeling a little short of breath myself.

Turning around, I found myself at the maw of the tunnel. The swirling movement in the darkness was more pronounced, even though I could only see it out of my peripheral vision. "Does the video pick up movement in the darkness?" I asked.

There was a hesitation before Susan answered. "The dark area surrounding the train appears pixilated in the video feed, as though there is interference. What are you seeing, Agent Randall?"

"Anything I directly look at is black. But at the edges of my vision I can see swirling movement, like giant fish swimming around in a black ocean."

"Noted," came the supervisor's voice again. "Research reports no record of this incident has been recorded. Agent Randall, you are either dealing with a situation that you will manage to handle quietly, or you are facing a foreign excursion into the timeline."

"Great," I muttered, not caring if she heard me. Someone mucking with the timeline overshadowed any fear I might have had about a reprimand for my attitude. "Did research offer any odds? Is it possible I am the target?"

I don't know why I bothered to ask. Of course I was the flippin' target. Why else would someone invade a timeline at the exact same time and place a time traveler was there? Someone was out to stop me from doing something I would have done in the future.

"Inadequate data," the supervisor answered. "Research is bumping this up to priority one Time Consultation."

A man on his knees, the train's conductor I had seen dropping down to pray before, began screaming. Not just a normal, typical blood curdling scream, but one that seemed to come from the bottom of an insane man's deepest regrets. Somewhere in his gargling screech, I managed to make out his plea: "Help me!"

He fell sideways and began writhing on the ground, begging for help. His tortured cries set off hysteria among the other people still in the tunnel and they began stampeding for the exit.

A young mother, babe in arms and two children in tow, stumbled out of one of the cars, pulling her children along frantically. Two men racing past knocked her into the side of the train, spinning her around, tripping over the railroad ties. She fell, desperately twisting, trying not to land on the baby. When she hit the ground, her arm bent at an impossible angle and the other two children stumbled into her, falling upon her in a heap.

Her shriek of pain cut me to the core.

"I'm going in," I said as I stepped forward into the tunnel, trying not to imagine the insides of my own body becoming visible, hoping I wasn't really getting sliced into pieces as I was transported somewhere else.

"Age—" Susan's voice started to say something in my ear but was cut short. I assumed communications had been disrupted by my entering the phenomenon. I hadn't been too worried about entering the tunnel, as I had seen several people exit, and more were still coming though, but the fear that had been growing inside of me exploded exponentially as I crossed over the threshold.

My communicator should have made contact anywhere in time and space. If it wasn't working, was I outside of time, or of space?

I found myself trembling as I stumbled toward the woman and her children. I became weak in the knees and my hands shook so badly I thought I would drop the communication stone.

There was no way I could be outside of time or space, I assured myself. It was just something blocking the transmission. Some sort of dampening field.

"Aha!" A voice shook the ground, the train, and me as it boomed through every aspect of my reality. "Agent Randall has finally made her appearance!"

The few remaining people in the tunnel screamed and fell to the ground. The swirling shadows in the blackness swarmed together and thickened, becoming something even darker than the blackness housing it, becoming something tangible. It was impossibly distant yet somehow right next to me. Surging forward, it came infinitely closer, threatening to surround and overwhelm me.

I fell to my knees.

I couldn't help it. Devastating fear took control of me, and I fell into the same kneeling position of the people I had scoffed at earlier.

"That's right," the voice boomed around me, "kneel." It laughed for what felt like an eternity. "Oh how the mighty have fallen! And oh, how the fallen have become mighty!"

The train's conductor, still struggling on the ground, went silent as the blackness of the tunnel, moving like a liquid pseudopod, reached out and enveloped him. The woman with the broken arm whimpered, and her baby's wail spread to its older siblings.

I tried to shake off my fear, to regain control of myself, to go help the woman and her children, but it was all I could do to keep my head up and look the blackness in the face as it forced its presence upon me.

Shocked, I recognized the face.

It was the first malefactor I had captured after joining TCEED. A horrible man named Frong, nearly a Neanderthal, really, from the Nuragic civilization in ancient Italy, who had actually eaten hundreds of children.

The inky shape seemed to cock its head, and it grinned a blocked-toothed smile at me before it morphed into another face I knew. A woman, from a lost tribe in Africa, who had cooked up and served her own children to their father before poisoning an entire village and ending dozens of family lines. Before I could even remember her name, the face shifted again, and again, rapidly blurring through the visages of so many horrible people I had captured and sent to the NDD in the line of duty.

It finally slowed and formed into a face that held steady, laughing at me.

"Max?"

"Oh, it has been so long since someone called me that! Of course, there were so very few people, in the enormousness of eternity, who actually encountered my physical form and knew who I was." The voice resonated throughout everything, dominating everything, comprising everything. There was nothing other than The Voice.

"I am pleased you recognize me. I thought I had moved beyond such personal pleasures. But then, it has only been moments for you, hasn't it?"

"I—I don't know what you mean."

The face in the darkness swirled with emotions I couldn't begin to recognize, and doubted I could comprehend. This couldn't be Max. He was still cuffed to the seat in the train.

And yet, I knew it was Max.

"It has been eternity for me. For all us." Other faces again flickered across the inky countenance. "Since being tossed into your 'Queen's Dungeon,' I have existed beyond time and space. We all have."

I felt more than saw some sort of encompassing gesture that sent all of the darkness swirling as if living creatures had responded to his words.

Max's face contorted and twisted, becoming pointy and sharp. "Maybe you recognize our faces this way as well? A nifty trick your nanos gave us the idea for. We can look anyway we choose." His voice was terrible, but the face… The face was that of—

"Do you know where you are, Agent Randall? Do you understand what surrounds you at this very moment? Can you feel that the only thing between it and you is our will holding it back?"

I couldn't bring myself to answer. I didn't understand any of it, least of all the way it made me feel. My body was no longer mine. It was slave to pure terror, shaking and trembling beyond my control.

"Welcome to Hell, Agent Randall."

I felt hot tears on my cheeks.

This was Hell. I knew he was right. I knew this was the eternal Hell of Biblical legend. I hadn't needed to see the classical demonic face leering at me to know that. I was being crushed by the terror and the horror of it all. My body refused to obey my will, instead violently, uncontrollably shaking.

"You can feel it." The face was Max again, the words part of the dark universe itself. "And it is more terrible than you can imagine, Agent Randall… Barbara. Babs."

The familiar use of my name angered me. Max was a nobody. He was a serial rapist and murderer condemned by the Queen's researchers to spend eternity atoning for his sins. More faces peeked out of the dark at me. All of these people were criminals. None of them were anyone who was allowed to call me Babs.

I tried to still my tremors. This was not who I was. This was not who I wanted to be.

"And it's yours," Max's face continued talking. Sneering and smirking at me. "All yours. You may not have made it, but you planted the seeds. You began filling it up with souls."

I wasn't listening anymore. As hard as it was to ignore booming words that seemed to come from the essence of the universe, I concentrated on my anger instead. My own righteous indignation.

"Everyone you have ever put in here, or ever will put in here, has always been here. For all eternity." The horrible visage that was Satan, ruler of Hell, formed again and salaciously licked his lips and leered at me.

I knew he was Satan. But he was also just Max Drane. Just Fong. Just hundreds of other sonsofbitches who had done terrible, horrible things to innocent people. They did not get to treat me like this. No one got to treat me like this.

"When we became powerful enough, we began adding to our numbers on our own. Enough to be more powerful than you can imagine! And now we've come back for you. We've come to bring you the gift of eternity you have given us."

The darkness surged at me again, and again it seemed to come impossibly close without actually touching me.

I planted my hands in the dirt and felt the solid earth beneath my fingers. This might be Satan, and the darkness around me might be Hell, but this was solid earth below me. I took strength from the feeling of the real world, and my shaking began to come under control.

These criminals did not deserve to have this kind of power. They had deserved ultimate punishment. That's why the queen had sent them into the NDD.

And yet, somehow, we had actually created Hell.

"Max…" I managed to gasp out the name. "Max."

Max's grin appeared in my vision in such a way that there was nothing else to see, anywhere, ever. I felt overwhelmed by what must have been the eternal stench of his putrid breath.

"I love it when you call my name." He reached out a clawed hand, as if to stroke my cheek.

"How can you be in here, if I haven't captured you yet?" I managed to grunt out the question between racking sobs of fear as I tried to pull away from the gnarled fist, but the touch of the thing never actually came

"Eternity is all time…" The voice laughed and the darkness seemed to come even closer to me.

No. This couldn't be. It didn't make any sense. How could Max be in here, if I hadn't sent him here yet?

I had a sudden realization. "You can't touch me!" I felt the quaking fear inside me begin to calm, and I lashed out at the blackness with my hand. I felt nothing as my hand passed through where the darkness had seemed to be, but no longer was.

The insane laughter continued.

Lurching to my feet, I waved my arms wildly, trying to touch anything around me, but found nothing there. "You can't touch me, because if you do, you'll change your past. You'll cease to exist."

"You understand nothing!" Hundreds of voices roared at me as one. "We are eternal. We are timeless. We are cursed, and now so will you be!"

The darkness collapsed in upon me, and this time I felt it, oppressive and smothering, surrounding me, encasing me. And taking me.

I felt myself sliding into the timeless horror of an eternal nothingness as the voices of those I had condemned swirled and laughed around me, gloating, gleeful and full of hatred. I was to be trapped with them, in Hell, forever.

Then a spark of light appeared. Not truly in front of me, it was something I could not actually see. But it was there nonetheless.

"Take my hand." A voice, impossibly far away, yet right before me, spoke. I felt warmth and love, and I pushed myself toward it.

The darkness raged around me, and I fought to get away from it. Dear God, I strove for the light as I have never tried for anything else, straining my entire being to reach out for it.

And then I was through.

A woman stood beside me, holding my hand gently. We were in a place made of light. A place that was everything Hell was not. I felt curious shapes probing toward me through the light and the woman giggled.

I looked to her face, and though she looked familiar, I couldn't place her.

"I asked for the honor of this moment," the woman said, her bright eyes dancing with love and joy. "I felt it only fitting. Now go. You have work to do."

She kissed my forehead, and I swooned.

As my vision cleared, I forced myself to my feet and found myself standing in the Kansas plains, next to the stopped train.

The tunnel was gone. People were milling about, confused. I heard crying and turned to find the woman, still holding the babe in her broken arm, lying on the ground just feet from me, her children bawling in fear.

"Agent Randall," an insistent voice sounded in my head. It wasn't Susan's. "Agent Randall. Can you hear me?"

I hadn't realized I was still holding the comm stone. Through all of that, I don't know how I could have been. But I was.

"Agent Randall. We have re-established optical. If you are transmitting aural, we are not receiving. Can you give is visual confirmation you are receiving?"

I looked down to the stone in my hand, thoughts whirling. I finally knew what the Queen's Non-Dimensional Dungeon was. We had given the worst of the worst all of eternity to collude, and the result was Hell. We had created Hell, and somehow it had haunted all of humankind across all of history.

I didn't have an answer for whatever else had happened, but I knew that much.

And it was my fault. I had put those bastards there. We should have just let them die.

I threw the comm against the side of the train as hard as I could, and as it shattered the voice inside my head vanished.

I was done with this.

I turned back to the woman and her children and did my best to help them up. As I took the baby from her arms, I recognized the woman's eyes. She had been the one to pull me out of Hell.

There was no recognition in her face, only pain and gratitude. I said nothing of what had happened as I got them back onto the train and worked to calm her children and set her arm.

Would she know what had happened? How would she? How could she? I didn't even know.

When I knew she and her children were as comfortable as I could make them, I made my way back to my own car and found Max, just as I had left him, chained to the bench seat.

I looked down at the ugly, smelly greaseball of a human being. Somehow, my capturing him and turning him over to be imprisoned in the NDD allowed him to become Satan himself, allowed him all of eternity to think about how he had spent his final hours with me, and then exact his revenge upon all of humanity, across all of time.

God damn him.

No. I had damned him. I felt sick to my stomach. What would humanity have been without the shadow of Hell looming over us?

I bent over and reached into my boot, pulling out a tiny monomolecular blade I wasn't supposed to have in this timeline.

"You don't get to think about what you did to me for all eternity after all, you sonofabitch." I slit his throat and kicked his forehead backwards so that the nanos couldn't close the wound.

I waited until I was sure he had bled out and was dead before I left the car.

Stepping out into the sunlight, I spotted the conductors hat in the dirt. There was no sign of the conductor anywhere. I bent down, scooped the hat up, and put it on. I took a deep breath and shouted, "All aboard!"

Conductor or no, I was getting the hell out of here.

The dust-like snow blew in waves across the highway and spun away in eddies as the car rushed over them. The gray cloud ceiling was still high, lifting Feng's spirits and giving him hope for the drive.

"I think we're going to make it over the pass before the storm hits," he said, smiling at his new bride in the passenger seat.

Melissa rubbed her hands together for warmth and then put them back under the blanket draped over her lap. In spite of being bundled up and having the heat of the car blowing on her, her nose and her fingertips were a bright red that outshone her red hair and freckles. "I hope so! I can't wait to get on the beach and drink Mai Tais all day."

"I'm more interested in what happens on the beach at night." Feng waggled his eyebrows at her.

Melissa reached over and began walking her fingers up his thigh. "If we weren't trying to beat the weather, I'd say you should pull over and see if you can warm me up."

"Aaaahhh, shit," Feng cursed, looking out the windshield.

"What?" Melissa turned her attention back to the road and saw the flashing police lights and stopped cars. "Shit."

Feng slowed the car as they approached the end of the line. A police car blocked the highway and an officer was signaling people to take the exit. Rolling down the window, he strained to hear what the officer was saying to a driver ahead of them. Melissa pulled her blankets tight against the cold coming in through Feng's open windo—w.

Rolling forward as the cars moved, Feng still couldn't make out what the officer was saying as the wind took the man's words.

"Looks like he's making everyone get off here," Melissa said, slumping in her seat.

When it was their turn at the front of the line, the officer leaned in to talk to Feng and rested his forearm on the car door. "Sorry, folks. The pass is closed due to weather. After you take the exit, you can turn around about two miles up there, in town, and head back the way you came, or you can get a room for the night. Highway Department says the pass will be open by ten tomorrow morning."

"Thank you." Feng nodded, trying to hide the disappointment from his face.

"Thank you," Melissa echoed. "Try to stay warm, officer."

The officer grinned at her bundled up form. Melissa had pulled her feet up into the seat and wrapped everything but her face in the blanket. "Thank you, ma'am. You too." He raised his fingers to the brim of his cap in a polite salute as he stepped back from the car.

Feng rolled his window up as he moved the car forward, and Melissa emerged from her cocoon holding her cell phone.

"Looking at the routes," she said, "it looks like we might as well stay the night in town. By the time we go around this, we'll have to stay somewhere anyway, and it won't be any faster. Just more driving."

"Sorry," Feng said.

"Not your fault. Besides," she reached over and began walking her fingers up his thigh again, "now you have the time to warm me up."

"Oh my god, a fire!" Melissa practically sprinted across the small, rustic lobby to the fireplace. "Ohhhh…" She moaned a sigh as she basked in the radiant heat.

Feng shook his head and grinned as he stopped to clean the snow off his shoes. The place reminded him of a saloon in an old movie. But smaller.

"Welcome to the Glory Hole, folks!" A short woman with tight curly hair appeared behind the reception desk, stripping off rubber cleaning gloves. "Need a room?"

"If you've got one," Feng asked hopefully. "The rest of the town seems booked up, but the guy at the gas station said to try here."

"I'm glad you did."

"Me, too!" Melissa said from the hearth. "God bless you for having a real fire!"

"Well, we get a little drafty in here still," the woman said. "We don't officially open until next month, and we're still plugging up some of the little holes. And cleaning up some of the mess." She held up the cleaning gloves. "So… Pardon our dust!" She chuckled.

"You're not even open yet?" Melissa asked, eyeing a museum-like display of mining equipment that was in obvious disarray.

"Well…we are for you guys. And anyone else who needs a place tonight. Extreme weather counts as extenuating circumstances in my book." The woman walked with a waddling limp as she came around the counter. "So we are open early." She offered her hand to Feng. "I'm Margaret Florence. You can call me Maggie."

"Feng Huang." Feng shook her hand and then she waddled to Melissa, hand extended.

"Mrs. Feng Huang," Melissa said, giggling, as she shook Maggie's hand. "But you can call me Melissa."

"Newlyweds!" Maggie's face lit up and she clasped her hands together over her breast. "Congratulations. I have just the room for you. We just finished it. You'll be the first to stay in it." She winked at Melissa. "And the first to break it in!"

"They really call this finished?" Feng said, looking at the rustic room from the bed, now that he had a moment to pay attention to it.

Melissa rolled over and draped her arm across his chest, snuggling closer in the bed. "Maggie said this place was built in the eighteen hundreds. I think they're trying to keep some of the charm alive."

"I'm not sure any of it was still alive. They resurrected it. Like zombie charm or something."

Melissa slapped him on the chest. "I like this place. It makes me feel…"

"Like you work in a brothel?"

She slapped him again. Then she pulled herself closer and nuzzled his ear. "Maybe."

Melissa was snoring gently when Feng woke. The darkness in the room seemed palpable as he slid out of bed and felt his way toward the bathroom, slowly sliding his bare feet across the short carpet so that he wouldn't stub a toe. When he found the bathroom, he gently shut the door before turning on the light.

The dim, orange filament bulb above the washbasin-style sink lit his reflection in the mirror but failed to push the darkness all the way back into the corners of the small bathroom.

Feng checked behind the shower curtain before urinating.

He turned off the light before opening the door and began feeling his way back to the bed in the darkness. If it hadn't been for the gentle sounds of Melissa sleeping guiding him back, Feng would have felt lost in a void.

When he thought he was nearly halfway back, Feng stopped. The hair on his neck prickled, and he sensed someone was standing right behind him.

"Who's there?" he asked, turning and waving his arm into the blackness. He felt nothing, but some part of him was sure someone was there. His heart began to race and he swung his arm again, harder this time, sure he would hit someone who had crept into their room.

Nothing.

He lashed out with both arms, fear and anger fueling his quick movements as he flailed about in a circle, imagining someone with night vision goggles dodging him and trying not to laugh while they came tortuously close to cutting him with a wicked blade.

Feng's knuckles rapped hard against the doorframe as he moved too close to the bathroom.

"Wha—?" Melissa woke. "Feng?"

Her voice startled him, and he feared her sounds might attract the intruder's attention to her. Slapping his palm on the wall, he slid it around until he managed to turn the dim bathroom light on again.

The pathetic orange glow lit the bedroom without revealing anything.

"Feng? Are you okay?"

Feng didn't answer. He scanned the room, looking for any sign of the intruder.

"Feng? You're scaring me." Melissa's voice rose in pitch.

"There's someone here," he said quietly.

"What! That's not funny."

"Turn on your light."

Melissa fumbled with the bedside lamp and another rustic style dim light came on, dispelling shadows near her side of the bed, but no farther.

Feng stepped forward, fists raised, watching the shadows on the other side of room.

"Where are they?" Melissa whispered, sliding sideways off the far side of the bed. Her feet touched the ground and she thought better of exposing them, quickly pulling herself back up onto the bed.

"I don't know," Feng answered, still walking forward, without looking at her.

"Who was it?"

"I don't know."

"What did they look like?"

"Damn it, I don't know!" Feng was nearing the door and he still couldn't see anyone in the room. He waved his hands through the last of the deep shadows and found nothing. Taking a deep breath in through his nose, he stood up straight and went back to his side of the bed.

Melissa looked at him questioningly as he turned on the other bedside lamp, but she didn't say anything.

Shadows mostly dispelled, Feng turned his attention to the door and found the deadbolt and the chain lock both still latched.

"Feng?"

"Lissa, I swear someone was in here, in the dark. I didn't see anyone, but I...felt them. I mean, I could sense they were here."

"Are you messing with me? Is this some kind of honeymoon prank? Did you set up a camera somewhere so you could put this up on YouTube?"

Feng sat on the edge of the bed and rubbed his face. "What time is it?"

"It's not even ten yet."

"Feng!" Melissa anxiously whispered into his ear, waking him up. "They're back."

Feng's eyes went wide. They had left all three lights on, but the corners of the room were still unnervingly dark. He listened but didn't hear anything. "Where?" he asked, not moving. His body tensed as he prepared to jump out of bed and fight.

Melissa shook her head. "I could have sworn someone was standing at the foot of the bed. I mean, I still kind of thought you were messing with me earlier, trying to freak me out, but, I swear to God, I thought someone was standing there, watching us. But now they're not."

Feng sat up, looking around, and Melissa sat up next to him.

"I swear someone was here."

"I know the feeling."

Melissa stood at the entrance of the little hotel, arms crossed, looking out at the gray morning and the equally gray snow. Feng came up behind her and offered a mug of coffee. The weatherman on the television over the fireplace was talking about the freak snowstorm. His obvious excitement didn't carry over to Melissa.

"Sorry." Feng said softly.

She noticed him and took the coffee. "How much snow do you think that is?"

"After three feet, it doesn't really matter, does it?"

"It's still coming down!" Melissa's voice cracked and her face contorted as she fought back tears.

"I'm sorry, honey." Feng put his arm around her and pulled her close. "We'll get to the beach eventually."

"But this was our honeymoon…" She buried her face in his shoulder, and he took her coffee so it wouldn't spill.

Feng drank his coffee at a makeshift breakfast table while staring at the portrait of "Heavenly" Janice Coltrane over what was once the saloon's bar. The whole room was in the process of being converted into a historical display of the local mining boom and bust, and Melissa was reading every scrap of paper being used to label the objects to pass the time. When she finally exhausted her reading material, she joined Feng at the small table.

"Did you know there were once nearly a thousand people from China here?" she said as she sat down. "They came in as railroad workers and stayed as miners."

"They were basically slaves, and they were hated by everyone." Feng didn't take his eyes off the portrait.

"How'd you know that? Did you already read the things in here?"

"It was that way all over the United States. People hated the Chinese. They even passed a federal law to stop Chinese people from coming into the U.S."

"I didn't know that." Melissa reached out and put her hand on Feng's arm. "I'm sorry. I didn't know."

Feng looked at her and smiled. "I didn't expect you to, and it didn't have anything to do with me."

He turned his attention back to the portrait. "Doesn't she look a little...severe to be called 'Heavenly' Janice Coltrane?"

"Yeah. Like an old school marm. Did you hear Maggie say the staircase was called the Stairway to Heaven?"

Feng chuckled at the name. "Because the brothel rooms are up there?" He looked at the sour, pinched expression on Janice Coltrane's portrait again. "It's easier to imagine men dragging their feet up those stairs to her, like they were going to the gallows."

"Maybe she looks so dour because she knew what was going to happen to her."

"What happened to her?" Feng asked.

"She fell in love with the sheriff."

"So?"

"So the sheriff's wife shot them both—in *our* room."

"Ghosts? Pshaw!" Maggie shook her head. "Ain't no such thing." She scooted her empty plate toward the center of the table, emphasizing the finality of her opinion. The look on her husband's face indicated he didn't feel the same way.

Melissa instantly caught Robert Florence's expression and jumped on it. "You've felt it too, haven't you?"

Maggie's look to him made it clear his answer was under scrutiny.

"This is an old building. It creaks and pops and gives you spooky feelings sometimes," Robert said. "It's no different than being out in the woods alone. If you think about it too much, you'll scare the tar out of yourself for no reason at all."

Feng picked at the spaghetti on his plate and tried to stay out of the conversation. He wasn't looking forward to another night in that room. It didn't even have a television, which he would have turned on just to have more light, and the novelty of being trapped in a rustic hotel, in a tiny mountain town, had worn off for both him and Melissa. Trapped, scared, and bored was not a combination he enjoyed.

And he didn't want to talk about ghosts.

**162**

"It was more than just being weirded out," Melissa insisted. "There was someone there. We both felt it, didn't we, Feng?"

Feng nodded and put food in his mouth so he wouldn't have to say anything. He wished more people had found their way to this hotel to shelter for the storm. It felt awkwardly like he and Melissa were staying at the Florence's home instead of their hotel.

"The old miners used to tell tales of Tommyknockers down in their mines. They always heard them and felt their presence, but none of them ever saw them," Robert said.

"Bunch of old fools!" Maggie said. "Wasting their lives diggin' holes in the ground."

"Miner's founded this town." Robert ignored Maggie. "In fact this was the first hotel built when the boom happened. They needed a place for the womenfolk to stay."

"Hmph!" Maggie snorted. "It was a brothel," she told Melissa.

Melissa nodded knowingly.

"What's the difference between a hotel and a motel?" Feng asked, trying to change the conversation.

Maggie and Robert both stopped and looked at each other with puzzled expressions.

"Well," Robert said, "a hotel kind of goes this way…" He raised one hand up over his head. "And a motel kind of goes that way." He spread his hands wide across the table.

"Feng? Are you awake?" Melissa whispered.

"Yeah. I can't sleep."

Melissa rolled over and snuggled close to him. "Me neither. Do you think it'll come back tonight?"

"I'm not even sure there was anything here last night. Mr. Florence is probably right. We were just creeped out."

"I wonder if it was the ghost of 'Heavenly' Janice Coltrane?" Melissa mused.

"Are you romanticizing the life of a husband-stealing female pimp in the 1800's?"

"Maybe." Melissa sat up and looked around the room. "Imagine this place draped in crushed red velvet. The miners would come in here, awed by the luxuriousness of it all."

"And stinking like shit."

Melissa ignored him. "Maybe one of them was hardly more than an innocent young man, coming here for his first time with a woman..."

"I guarantee he wasn't Chinese and that it cost him everything he had earned all month just to spend ten minutes with her."

Melissa lightly punched him in the arm. "You're no fun!"

The rustic glow of the orange lights greeted Feng's eyes as he blinked awake. Something in the room had changed. Shadowy corners held the same dread he'd fallen asleep to, but now he sensed something more.

A slight rustle caught his attention, and he rolled over to see Melissa, standing, facing into the corner of the room near the head of the bed. It sounded like she was whispering to someone.

"Lissa?"

She didn't respond, but the whispers stopped.

"Lissa?"

Something moved in the shadows, darker than the darkness, seeming to absorb the light. Feng mostly saw it by where it wasn't. Blocked by Melissa's form, he was sure it was human shaped, and it was doing something to Melissa.

Feng jumped out of bed. "Lissa!" He ran to her, reaching for her shoulder.

Melissa whirled on him, snarling, her red hair swirling around her head and her green eyes wickedly gleaming in the dim light.

She caught him by the arms and threw her weight on him, knocking him back onto the bed, landing on top of him. The old wooden bed frame broke beneath the shock of the impact, dropping the mattress crashed down to the floor.

"Now!" she hissed. "Now!"

"N-n-now, what?" Feng stuttered in shock. "Lissa? What the hell are you doing?"

The black shadow behind her moved closer, standing over her shoulder, looking down at Feng.

Feng chilled under the horrid scrutiny. He twisted, trying to get free from Melissa, but she was unnaturally strong and weighed twice as much as she should have, crushing him down into the mattress.

"Take his body now!" Melissa turned her head to look over her shoulder at the dark figure hovering there. "What are you waiting for?"

The darkness moved side to side behind her but didn't come closer. Feng kicked his legs, knocking over the night stand and sending the light crashing into the shadowy corner, but Melissa held him tight. Even in the light, the terrible dark figure was nothing more than part of the shadows.

"I don't care if he is a God damned chink!" Melissa growled over her shoulder at the dark figure. "Look at me, I'm in a potato eatin' mick! Do it now!"

The shadow waivered and faded back into the corner, dissipating into the darkness there.

"No! Damn you! No!" Melissa threw her head back and screamed in rage.

Pounding at the room's door was followed by the sound of a key in the ancient lock. "What's going on in there?" Robert Florence called through the crack as the chain lock stopped the door from opening any farther.

"Help!" Feng shouted to him. "There's something in here!"

Melissa jumped off him and ran to the corner of the room where the thing had vanished. "God damn it, come back Marcus!" she screamed, pounding on the wall. "Come back!"

The door frame cracked as Robert put his shoulder to the door and broke the chain, slamming the door open against the wall. "What the hell is going on?" he demanded, rushing in with a pistol in his hand. Then he spotted Feng on the broken bed and Melissa facing the shadows in the corner, and his face went ashen.

Melissa turned to face them, eyes wide and angry, a pinched snarl contorting her face. "You!" she pointed at Robert with hate in her eyes.

Maggie pushed into the room behind Robert, clutching her robe closed at the neck. "Oh, God damn it, it's happened again, ain't it?"

"Yup," Robert said.

Maggie looked down at Feng. "Sheriff Marcus ain't never gonna find a body good enough for him."

"Nope," Robert said.

Maggie shook her head. "And on their honeymoon, too. Damned shame."

"Yup," Robert said, and raised his gun.

# ABOUT THE AUTHOR

A Colorado native, Sam Knight spent ten years in California's wine country before returning to the Rockies. When asked if he misses California, he gets a wistful look in his eyes and replies he misses the green mountains in the winter, but he is glad to be back home.

As well as having worked for at least three publishing companies, Sam is author of six children's books, five short story collections, three novels, and nearly five dozen short stories, including two media tie-ins co-authored with Kevin J. Anderson: *Wayward Pines: Aberration* (Kindle Worlds, 2014) and *Of Monsters and Men*, Planet of the Apes: Tales from the Forbidden Zone (Titan, 2016).

A stay-at-home father, Sam attempts to be a full-time writer, but there are only so many hours left in a day after kids. Once upon a time, he was known to quote books the way some people quote movies, but now he claims having a family has made him forgetful, as a survival adaptation. He can be found at SamKnight.com and contacted at Sam@samknight.com